"Come here, Jess."

Quinn's voice was unusually husky as he extended his hand toward her.

As if in a trance, Jessica reached out, allowing her hand to be swallowed in his. A second later she was in his arms, fitted intimately against him. A warmth suffused her, making her breasts ache with unaccustomed heaviness.

"Ah, Jess," Quinn murmured, burying his lips in the fragrant softness of her hair. "I promised I wouldn't push, but I'll go crazy if I can't make love to you."

She lifted her head, a slight smile teasing her lips. "What's stopping you?"

"Sweetheart," he groaned, "I thought you'd never ask...."

THE AUTHOR

JoAnn Ross lives in Arizona with her husband and teenage son. A prolific writer, she has been published under her own name as well as the pseudonyms JoAnn Robb and JoAnn Robbins.

Without Precedent is set in JoAnn's favorite city, San Francisco. It's one of the most romantic spots in the world, she asserts. Just perfect for a love story.

Recent Books by JoAnn Ross

HARLEQUIN TEMPTATION

67—LOVE THY NEIGHBOR
77—DUSKFIRE

HARLEQUIN INTRIGUE

27—RISKY PLEASURE

These books may be available at your local bookseller.

Don't miss any of our special offers. Write to us at the following address for information on our newest releases.

Harlequin Reader Service
901 Fuhrmann Blvd.,
P.O. Box 1325, Buffalo, N.Y. 14269
Canadian address: P.O. Box 2800, Postal Station A,
5170 Yonge St., Willowdale, Ont. M2N 6J3

Without Precedent

JOANN ROSS

Harlequin Books

TORONTO • NEW YORK • LONDON
AMSTERDAM • PARIS • SYDNEY • HAMBURG
STOCKHOLM • ATHENS • TOKYO • MILAN

To Robin Lester, for her enthusiastic support,
and Gerry Griner, the other woman in my
husband's life.

Published February 1986

ISBN 0-373-25196-3

1

FORCING HERSELF TO IGNORE the thousands of hot needles pricking her legs, Jessica O'Neill reminded herself that pain was all in the mind. The fact that her thighs felt as if they were on fire was merely a temporary mental aberration. While Jessica had been repeating that axiom for the last four blocks, the words were beginning to ring false, even to her own ears.

Only a fool took up jogging on San Francisco's hilly streets, she considered, urging her weary body back to her Haight Ashbury town house. Or a masochist. Jessica decided she was probably a little of both. She dragged herself up the concrete steps and leaned against the bright blue siding, gasping for breath. Just then she heard the telephone ring. And ring. And ring.

"For Pete's sake," she muttered, flinging open the screen door, "you'd think someone could answer the damn phone."

Her rubbery legs proved scant support, and intent on reaching the telephone, Jessica failed to notice the matching set of Louis Vuitton luggage in the foyer. She tripped, sprawling ignominiously over the oak flooring. The strident demand of the telephone was unceasing, and giving up on walking for the moment, Jessica crawled the rest of the way into the front parlor of her Victorian home.

"Jill," she shouted upstairs to her eldest daughter, "turn down that music! Hello?" she got out, lying on her back, gasping like a grounded trout, her breath stirring her unruly auburn bangs. The room was suddenly bathed in a brilliant light as an eleven-year-old girl aimed a video camera at her.

"Knock it off," Jessica snapped, scowling into the camera lens.

There was a stunned silence on the other end of the phone. "Are you talking to me?" a hesitant female voice finally asked.

Jessica was still waving her hand at the whirring camera. "No, not at all.... Mallory Anne O'Neill, get out of here," she hissed at the aspiring cinematographer.

The caller's voice was a frantic combination of a screech and a sob. "You have to do something!"

Now what? Jessica sighed as she struggled to a sitting position. "Jill!" she shouted again, covering the mouthpiece with her palm before returning to her hysterical client. "Mrs. Thacker? What's the problem?"

"It's Keith!" the woman wailed.

Vowing never to handle divorce cases once her law career was established, Jessica closed her eyes, garnering strength to continue this conversation. "What's he done now?"

"I can't believe it! Mrs. O'Neill, I want that man arrested. Right now!"

"Mrs. Thacker," Jessica crooned in a calm, authoritative voice, "why don't you take a deep breath and start at the beginning?"

A sound like a steam engine came across the line as the woman obviously followed Jessica's advice. "It's my Mercedes," she said finally in a voice that cracked slightly, but was at least understandable.

"He had it stolen," Jessica guessed.

She was at her wit's end with the antics of Mr. and Mrs. Thacker. Jessica empathized with her client—what discarded ex-wife wouldn't—but the term "civilized divorce" was obviously not in the Thackers' vocabulary.

"I only wish he had," Sylvia Thacker wailed, her voice high enough to shatter glass. "Then at least it would still be in one piece.... The bastard cut it in half. With a hacksaw!"

"A hacksaw?" Jessica arched an auburn brow. "Is that even possible?"

"He left the saw behind. Shall I call the police?"

"Let me handle it," Jessica suggested. "I'm certain if I contact your husband's attorney, we can settle this without pressing charges."

"I'd rather see the creep in jail," the woman muttered.

"I'm certain you would. But if we press charges for this act of vandalism, you may end up behind bars yourself. He could always countersue for your little display of temper last week."

The tears stopped abruptly as Jessica's client recovered her poise. "I thought you were supposed to be on my side, Mrs. O'Neill. Mr. Bennington assured me that you were quite capable of handling my divorce."

The threat was sheathed in silk, but Jessica recognized it for what it was. Mrs. Sylvia Thacker née Montgomery, came from one of San Francisco's oldest families. One suggestion to the head of Bennington, Marston, White and Lowell that the newest member of the firm was not treating a valued client with due respect and Jessica would be lucky to end up working in the public defender's office.

"Of course I'm on your side," she said quickly. "And if you're certain you'll be all right, I'll hang up now and contact your husband's attorney immediately."

"Tell him that if I catch that worm of an ex-husband on my property, I'm going to shoot first and ask questions later," Sylvia Thacker warned.

"Please don't do that, Mrs. Thacker. I'm sure we can all come to an amicable settlement."

"Terrific. Now I've got Pollyanna representing me," the woman muttered as she hung up the phone.

Jessica went onto her knees, riffling through her Roledex on the cluttered desk top. "Marston...Martin...Masterson. Quinn Masterson, you'd better still be in your office," she mumbled, knowing it to be a long shot. It was past seven o'clock, and if the man's reputation was halfway warranted, he usually spent his evenings in far more pleasurable pursuits than working on legal briefs.

His answering service confirmed Jessica's suspicions. The woman agreed to try to get a message to Mr. Masterson, but her bored tone didn't give Jessica a great deal of confidence. She was debating what to do next when her eye caught an invitation she'd glanced at and dismissed several weeks ago. The San Francisco Committee for the Preservation of the Arts was having a fund raising ball at the Fairmont Hotel. The chairman of the ball was none other than Quinn Masterson. As Jessica read the date on the invitation, she decided her luck was looking up.

"Mrs. Thacker's having trouble with her husband again, right?" The youthful voice cut through her musings.

In the midst of her client's problem, Jessica had forgotten all about the video camera still trained on her. "Put that thing down," she instructed firmly. "I'm getting sick and tired of living in a goldfish bowl."

Blue eyes as wide and vivid as Jessica's held her mother's stern gaze with implacable purpose. "It's my class project. Do you want me to fail?"

"I want you to find another project," Jessica snapped. "Whatever happened to rock collections? Or Styrofoam models of the moon?"

"I'm doing a sociological study of a family in transition," Mallory O'Neill stated resolutely. "You'll love it."

"I doubt that, since I already hate it," Jessica countered, raising her voice to be heard over the throbbing beat of rock music. "Jill," she called, going in search of her eldest daughter. "I'm going out."

Jessica followed the sound to the upstairs bedroom shared by two of her three daughters where she found her thirteen-year-old lipsyncing to the latest Cyndi Lauper record.

"Hey!" Jill protested as Jessica lifted the needle. "I'm rehearsing for Mallory's movie!"

"That shows how much you know about cinema vérité," Mallory sniffed, still filming the confrontation. "It's true life, dummy. You're not supposed to rehearse. Boy, are some people dumb!"

"Mallory, if you don't put that camera down right now, you're going to have your first experience with censorship," Jessica warned. "And, Jill, from now on, when I'm conducting business at home, I'd prefer to forego the background music, okay?"

Her daughter shrugged, irritating Jessica unreasonably as she blew an enormous pink bubble through pursed lips.

"Sure, Mom," she agreed nonchalantly. "But I didn't hear the phone ring."

"I'm not surprised since the noise level in this room was somewhere between a jackhammer and the Concorde. Where's Sara?" she asked belatedly, realizing that she hadn't seen the youngest O'Neill daughter.

"Sara's out shopping with Gran."

"Gran?"

"Yeah. Gran says everything in our refrigerator is loaded with additives."

"I don't see where my additives are any of your grandmother's concern. Mallory, turn that camera off!"

"I don't want to miss your expression when you hear the news," Mallory argued.

"News? What news?"

"Gran's moving in with us," Jill answered her mother.

Jessica blinked, forgetting the whirring camera capturing her stunned reaction. "In here? In this house?"

Mallory bobbed her strawberry blond head in the affirmative. "Isn't that neat? She's bound to get me an A on my project. Just think, three generations of women living in the same house, all experiencing the slings and arrows of divorce."

"That's ridiculous," Jessica returned instantly. "Your grandmother has been married forty-six years. She'd never get a divorce."

"That's not what she said," Mallory put in. "Tell her, Jill."

"She says she's left Gramps," Jill confirmed.

Before Jessica could answer, the phone began to ring again. "That's going to be Mrs. Thacker," Jessica said with a sigh. "Jill, tell her I've gone to meet with Mr. Masterson." She spun around, fixing her middle daughter with a stern glare. "And turn that thing off!"

"All right," Mallory muttered, reluctantly lowering the camera. She spoke quietly in deference to Jill's conversation. "But I would have loved to show how adults make their kids lie for them."

"It was her," Jill acknowledged, hanging up the phone. "Are you really going out?"

"I've got to," Jessica said reluctantly, the idea not on her hit parade of things to do with a rare free evening. "But there's plenty of stuff in the freezer for you to heat up in the microwave for dinner. I shouldn't be long."

"Are you going out like that?"

Jill's voice was laced with teenage scorn as she eyed Jessica's pink sweat suit. Jessica, in turn, fixed her daughter with a slow, appraising look, taking in the dark hair slicked back with styling gel, the neon orange sweatshirt, kelly green vinyl pants and suede boots.

"You're a fine one to talk, kiddo," she said. "I figure if I can put up with the punk look, you can survive a mother who has more important priorities than looking like a fashion plate." Jessica grinned over her shoulder as she left the room. "Tell your grandmother I won't be late. She's got some heavy explaining to do."

"Radical!" Mallory clapped her hands. "I just know I'm going to get an A this year."

"Off the record," Jessica warned, wagging her finger. "I don't want this family's private lives dragged through your junior high school."

"We've already had our lives dragged through the press," Mallory pointed out with deadly accuracy. "This at least will be the truth."

From the mouths of babes, Jessica considered as she took the bus to the Fairmont Hotel atop Nob Hill. She'd done her best to protect the girls when the news of her divorce had hit the papers, but, after all, Brián O'Neill had been in the public eye for some time, including his unsuccessful campaign for governor of California. When the word got out that he'd left his family for another woman, the spotlight had shifted to Jessica and her three daughters. Fortunately, a story about graft payments to certain members of the city council had drawn the attention away from them, allowing a fairly normal existence the past three years. Although it certainly wasn't the luxurious Marin County life they were used to, Jessica privately thought the changes had done them all good.

She smiled at the liveried doorman, ignoring his arched brow at her attire as she entered the elegant hotel. Looking neither right nor left, Jessica crossed the thick black-and-red lobby carpeting to the desk.

"May I help you?" The young man looked doubtful, but his polite, professional smile didn't waver.

"I'm looking for the Arts ball," Jessica explained.

"It's in the main ballroom, but—"

Jessica gave him a dazzling smile. "Thank you very much," she said, heading off in the direction he'd just indicated.

QUINN MASTERSON was bored stiff. He'd always hated these things and, at age forty, was beginning to lose patience with the pretence that he found them at all enjoyable. While he understood the need for charitable organizations, and the necessity of well-meaning individuals to direct them, he'd never gotten to the point that he felt comfortable. As he nodded at the clutch of women around him, hoping that he was answering with the proper phrases at the appropriate times, he wondered if they ever suspected he felt totally out of place in the luxurious ballroom, surrounded by all these glittering people.

Face it, Masterson, he told himself. *Deep down, you're still that Missouri farm boy struggling to learn the two-step.* His bored gaze circled the room, looking for someone, anyone, he could carry on an interesting conversation with.

His green eyes locked on the slender woman standing in the doorway. She certainly didn't belong here, he mused, eyeing her pink running suit, which stood out like a sore thumb amid the sequined and beaded gowns of the other women in the room. Her auburn hair had sprung free of the ribbon at the back of her neck, creating a brilliant halo around her head that he found far more enticing than the stiff, well-coiffed hairdos of the women surrounding him. Some distant memory tried to make itself known in his mind, but Quinn had no time to dwell on it now.

She was obviously arguing with the man taking tickets at the door, but while she appeared determined, Quinn had the impression that this was not a lady used to making a scene. What was she doing here? While no answer came immediately to mind, Quinn had every intention of finding out.

She'd piqued his interest, and it had been a very long time since a woman had done that. His mind went into gear as he tried to come up with some way to escape this inane conversation before she got away.

"No, I don't have a ticket," Jessica told the guardian of the door for the third time. "I've no intention of attending the ball. I only want to speak with Mr. Masterson."

"I can't let you in without a ticket, ma'am," the elderly man stated firmly. "Those are the rules."

"Oh, for heaven's sake," Jessica huffed, her breath feathering her curly bangs. "This is ridiculous!" She watched as three more couples handed over their five-hundred-dollar tickets and achieved immediate access. Then an outrageous idea occurred to her.

"Excuse me," she stated sweetly, "but it is very important that I speak with Mr. Masterson."

"I've already explained—"

Jessica's blue eyes were absolutely guileless. "I know—the rules. But would it be breaking those rules if I asked you to take a message to Mr. Masterson for me?"

He rubbed his jaw. "I don't know."

"It's a very short message," she coaxed.

"I don't see where any harm would be done by that," he allowed.

"Thank you." Jessica rewarded him with her prettiest smile. Leaning forward, she placed her palm on his arm and lowered her voice slightly. "Would you please tell Mr. Masterson that Trixie is here with her cheerleader outfit and needs to know if he wants her to wait up in his room, as usual."

Jessica's expression was absolutely bland as she ignored the gasp of a couple who had just arrived. The ticket taker's face blossomed to a hue rivaling a lobster's, and his eyes widened as they took a jerky tour of her body, clad in the soft cotton jersey.

"Why don't I just get Mr. Masterson for you and let you deliver the message in person," he suggested.

Jessica nodded. "Thank you," she agreed sweetly.

Quinn had just about decided to forego social tenets and walk away from the quintet of babbling women when he was rescued by the doorman.

"Excuse me, Mr. Masterson, but there's someone here who insists on speaking with you."

Quinn's eyes cut to the doorway where the woman still waited. Her blue eyes were directed his way and for a long, timeless interval their gazes held, exchanging any number of messages, each one more personal than the previous. He couldn't believe his luck.

Jessica recognized the man instantly. Quinn Masterson's picture had appeared on the cover of innumerable magazines. He also showed up regularly in newspapers and on television. But none of those mediums had captured the essence of the man.

He was gorgeous, she admitted reluctantly. Thick, sun-gilt gold hair fell over a broad forehead. His eyes were bright green and seemed to light with something akin to recognition as he came toward her.

"You must be a genie," he stated immediately, his emerald eyes warming provocatively.

Jessica hadn't missed the gleam of appreciation in his gaze as he'd stared at her from across the room. While she knew she was no beauty, she still received her share of appreciative glances from men, even if Jill did consider her thirty-five-year-old mother "over the hill." Under normal situations, Jessica liked being found attractive. What had shaken her to her toes was the fact Quinn Masterson had stirred something long forgotten within her.

"A genie?" she asked blankly, ignoring his outstretched hand.

"There I was, wishing for you, when you popped up. Just like that." He snapped his fingers.

"Not exactly just like that," she countered, unreasonably irritated by his boyish smile. "I'm here to find out what you're going to do about your client sawing a brand-new Mercedes in half with a hacksaw."

Quinn arched a blond brow. "A hacksaw?"

"A hacksaw."

"I assume you're talking about Keith Thacker."

This was the woman Keith Thacker consistently described as an ill-tempered harridan? While Quinn had known Keith for years and knew of his wife's social status in the city, this was the first time he'd actually met Sylvia Thacker. Lord, he considered, staring down at her, while Keith could admittedly be accused of irrational behavior from time to time, letting this woman get away proved he was downright certifiable.

Jessica nodded, causing a few additional strands of unruly auburn hair to spring loose. "That's exactly who I'm talking about. You have to do something about your crazy client, Mr. Masterson. The man is literally driving me up a wall!"

Two red flags waved in her cheeks, revealing a barely restrained inner passion, and Quinn decided Keith was indeed crazy to leave this woman for that twenty-year-old art student. Although he usually attempted to convince his clients to try marriage counseling, Quinn knew he wasn't going to recommend that option this time. In fact, tomorrow morning he was going to call his old college buddy and inform him he couldn't handle the case. There would be a definite conflict of interest, since Quinn had every intention of winning Thacker's wife.

"Let's go somewhere quiet and talk about it," he suggested, cupping her elbow with his palm.

Jessica shook off his hand. "We can talk about it right here," she insisted. "Besides, aren't you needed in there?"

He waved off her concern. "Don't worry about it—they'll carry on without me just fine. Are you hungry? I know a little place in Chinatown that the tourists haven't discovered."

"Are you asking me to dinner?"

"Have you eaten?"

"No," Jessica admitted.

He grinned down at her. "Then I guess I am."

"I'm not dressed," she protested, suddenly feeling out of place in the glittering crowd. She'd been so angry when she'd come down here that the contrast in attire hadn't disturbed her. Now, seeing herself through Quinn Masterson's attractive green eyes, Jessica felt hopelessly disheveled.

"I think you look great," he argued. "I don't know many women with your hair color who'd dare to wear hot pink, but it sure works on you."

Instructing herself not to blush, Jessica dragged her mind back to business. "I'm here to discuss your client," she stated firmly, rocking back on the heels of her running shoes.

"And we will," he agreed, his palm pressed against her back as he urged her down the mirrored hallway. "Just as we'll discuss that little trick you pulled."

Jessica stopped in her tracks. "Trick?"

"Emptying the house while the poor guy was at work. That was playing dirty pool, Mrs. Thacker."

She stared up at him uncomprehendingly. "I'm not Mrs. Thacker."

Now Quinn was confused. "Then who are you?"

"Jessica O'Neill. Mrs. Thacker's attorney."

"I thought George Bennington was handling the divorce for her."

"He assigned it to me last week. Didn't you get my letter?"

"I've been out of town," he answered distractedly, as he attempted to remember exactly where he'd seen this woman before. "Jessica O'Neill," he mused aloud. "The name rings a bell."

"I'm not surprised," Jessica said dryly, waiting for the recognition to hit.

She didn't have to wait long. "You're Brian O'Neill's wife."

"Ex-wife," she corrected.

"Ex-wife," Quinn repeated, telling himself he shouldn't sound so damn happy about her marital status.

But he felt as if he'd been waiting for Jessica O'Neill all his life, and it was a distinct relief to discover she was available. Not that it would have mattered, of course. It only would have made things a bit messier if she'd had a husband out there somewhere.

"I suppose I should tell you I'm sorry," he said slowly.

Jessica merely shrugged in response.

"But I'm not going to," Quinn decided. "Because I've always had one firm rule in life."

"And that is?"

He reached out, tugging on a bright russet curl that kissed her cheek. "Never look a gift genie in the mouth."

It was only a few blocks from the Nob Hill hotel to the Chinatown restaurant and since the early spring night was unseasonably balmy, Quinn and Jessica decided to walk.

"What did you tell Ernie, anyway?" Quinn asked. "I've never seen the old guy's feathers as ruffled as they were when he came over with the good news that you'd come to the hotel tonight to see me."

Knowing that it wasn't going to do a lot for her professional image, Jessica nevertheless confessed, drawing a deep, appreciative laugh from Quinn, who proceeded to imitate the stuffy doorman perfectly. He continued to disprove the theory about lawyers being as dry as their documents by treating Jessica to a series of impersonations, spoofing some of the city's more illustrious individuals.

"You're terrible!" Jessica's blue eyes were gleaming with tears of laughter as Quinn portrayed an eccentric, left-wing councilman with uncanny accuracy.

"Hey," he complained with a grin. "I thought it was pretty good."

"It was," she admitted, forgetting for the time being that she had every reason to be furious with Quinn Masterson. His client's behavior had been unconscionable. "If you ever give up the law, you can always have a career in show business."

"A few clients like Keith Thacker and I'll consider it," he agreed. "A hacksaw?"

"That's what Sylvia claims." She gave him her sternest expression. "Now I suppose you're going to claim you had nothing to do with it."

The look had as little effect on Quinn as it did when she used it on the girls. Instead of being intimidated, he appeared wounded by her words.

"Me?" Quinn flung a hand innocently against his chest. "Are you really accusing me of using such tactics?"

Jessica honestly had her doubts, but although she had just taken on the case a few days ago, the couple had been driving her crazy. She couldn't help taking some of that frustration out on Quinn.

"What if I am?"

"Then, Ms O'Neill, I'd be forced to point out that what we have here is a case of the pot calling the kettle black. I suppose you didn't have anything to do with your client absconding with every last thing in their house the day before she filed for divorce?"

Jessica rose to her full height in an attempt to look him straight in the eye. Just under five foot six, she'd always considered herself reasonably tall, but Quinn was at least two inches over six feet. That, plus the fact she was wearing running shoes, put him at a distinct physical advantage.

"Of course I didn't. Besides Sylvia didn't take everything. She left his clothes."

"Which she cut to shreds."

"Touché," Jessica murmured. "Whatever happened to civilized divorces, anyway? Those two are driving me up the wall."

"You're not alone," Quinn muttered. "Do you think that's possible?" he asked suddenly.

"What?"

"Civilized divorces. Do you really believe a man or woman can give up someone they love without a lot of anger?"

"I did."

He stopped, looking down at her with a thoughtful expression. "If that was actually the case, perhaps you didn't really love your husband," he suggested.

"That's ridiculous," Jessica snapped, drawing her arms about herself in an unconscious gesture of self-protection.

How had they gotten on the topic of her ill-fated marriage, anyway? She didn't like discussing it with anyone; she damn well wasn't going to discuss it with a man who'd been voted San Francisco's most eligible bachelor so many times that he'd been elevated to the Hall of Fame.

"Besides," she said tightly, "what do you know about marriage?"

"Not much," he remarked. "But after fifteen years of practicing law, I know a hell of a lot about divorce. And it's rare when the parties involved don't end up at each other's throat."

"I didn't have any choice," Jessica found herself admitting softly. "I had three daughters I wanted to protect from being hurt any more than they were. Speaking of which, I need to let them know I'm not going to be home for dinner."

"You can phone from the restaurant," he assured her, his hand lightly on her back once again. Jessica tried to ignore how right his touch felt, how much she was enjoying his company.

Just then she made the mistake of glancing in a darkened store window, and her heart sank at her reflection. She looked at least ten pounds heavier in the jogging suit and her hair was a wild, unruly cloud springing out in all directions from her head. She looked as if she'd just gone ten rounds with Larry Holmes and felt like groaning at the contrast between her disheveled appearance and the formally dressed man beside her.

"Look," she stated suddenly, "this is a bad idea. I'm sorry I went off the deep end about the Mercedes—I believe you didn't know anything about it. Why don't I call you at your office tomorrow and we can work out a fair settlement?"

"What's the matter?" Quinn asked, his heart sinking as he viewed Jessica's determined expression. She was going to get away, after all. He vowed not to let that happen."

"I have to get home."

"Are your daughters alone?"

Jessica had always been a lousy liar and knew better than to try now with a man renowned for his ability to read a jury. "No," she admitted. "My mother's with them."

His grin practically split his tanned face. "Terrific. Then you don't have anything to worry about."

That's what you think, Jessica thought, trying to make sense of these errant feelings she'd been having since she and Quinn Masterson had exchanged that long look across the ballroom. It was too corny to be believed, but it was true. Something indefinable had passed between them, and Jessica was unwilling to pursue its cause.

"Jessie," he murmured, two long fingers cupping her chin to raise her eyes to his coaxing smile. "You wouldn't really leave me to eat alone, would you?"

"You weren't alone back there," she argued, tossing her head in the direction of the Fairmont.

"I felt alone."

"Oh." Jessica thought about that for a minute, understanding the feeling. She'd always felt like that on the campaign trail, even though she'd been continually surrounded by members of Brian's staff. "How do you feel now?" she asked softly.

Jessica was entranced by his broad, boyish grin. "I feel terrific." Then his expression suddenly turned unnervingly sober. "Please have dinner with me, Jessica. I can't remember when I've wanted anyone's company quite so much."

If it was a line, Jessica considered, it was certainly working. She didn't think she could have turned Quinn Masterson down if her life depended on it.

"I have to get home early," she warned.

"Don't worry, Cinderella," he stated with a bold, satisfied smile. "I promise to get you home before you turn into a pumpkin."

2

JESSICA WAS SURPRISED as Quinn led her up a set of back stairs to a small, intimate restaurant over a store filled with tourist paraphernalia. She'd grown up in San Francisco, but had never run across the Empress Pavilion.

"Is this place new?" she asked as they settled into a high-backed, private booth.

"No. Bruce Tso took over the management about five years ago when his mother retired. She ran the place for fifteen years before that."

"I've never heard of it."

Quinn grinned. "Once you taste the food, you'll see why Bruce doesn't have to advertise. Actually, it's off the beaten track for the tourists and lacks the celebrity status a lot of the natives require." He seemed to be studying her, waiting for her reaction.

Jessica silently compared his attitude toward dining with that of her ex-husband's. Eating with Brian O'Neill had been an occasion to be in the public eye; he'd never select a quiet, out-of-the-way spot like this. Which was one of the reasons they seldom went out together in the later years of their marriage. She'd disliked having her meal constantly interrupted by other diners who shared Brian's compulsion for table-hopping.

"I like it," she murmured.

Quinn visibly relaxed. "I thought you might. How adventuresome are you feeling tonight?"

Did he have to even ask? Here she was, practically picking up a strange man, agreeing to share an intimate meal while dressed like Little Orphan Annie. For a woman known to plan every waking hour of her day, she was definitely throwing caution to the winds.

"What did you have in mind?" she asked in a low, throaty voice. Good Lord, Jessica considered, was she actually flirting?

Quinn decided that if he was perfectly honest with her, she'd probably think he was certifiably crazy. She didn't look like a woman who'd believe in love at first sight. He had a vague feeling Jessica O'Neill was extremely practical and down-to-earth, under ordinary circumstances. But this was no ordinary night.

"The house specialty is Szechwan, but some of it is admittedly a little spicy for American palates."

Jessica laughed delightedly. "Does the chef know how to cook *la chiso ch'ao chi?* It's my favorite."

Quinn was not surprised to discover that Jessica shared his enjoyment of the spicy chicken sautéed with peppers. Accustomed to acting on instinct, he had known at first glance Jessica was precisely the person he'd been seeking.

Quinn had set a master plan for his life back in college. After law school he'd sign on with a prestigious firm, concentrating his energies on becoming one of the best legal brains in the country. And though he had no intention of living like a Trappist monk, neither was he going to allow himself to get involved while learning his craft. He would become a senior partner by the time he was forty; then, and only then, would he turn his energies to creating a family.

Well, he'd turned forty last month, he was a senior partner as planned, and it was time to concentrate on finding a wife. Quinn was pleased but not overly surprised by the fact that Jessica had shown up exactly on schedule. He'd always been lucky.

"You're going to love it here," he promised.

Jessica's gaze swept the room, taking in the enchanting Oriental atmosphere before settling on Quinn's handsome face. "I already do," she said.

Jessica was vaguely aware that the dinner Quinn had ordered was superb, but if anyone had asked her what she was eating, she wouldn't have been able to answer. All her attention was focused on Quinn Masterson—even on the smallest of details. She observed the unruly lock of blond hair that seemed destined to fall over his forehead, noted the way little lines fanned out attractively from the corners of his green eyes when he smiled at her, which was often. His deep baritone voice, she decided, seemed to be coming from inside a velvet-lined drum. Everything about him fascinated her, and Jessica was amazed when the waiter took their empty plates, bringing them a fresh pot of hot tea.

Taking a sip of the fragrant brew, Jessica lifted her eyes and was unnerved to find Quinn staring at her intently.

"I keep trying to remember where we've met," he admitted.

"We haven't."

"Of course we have," he corrected amiably. "I never forget a face. Especially not one as lovely as yours. Just give me a minute and I'll come up with it."

"You're wasting your time," she said firmly. "Watch my lips, Quinn. We've never—I repeat, never—met. You're undoubtedly remembering me from the news coverage of the campaign."

"Nice," he murmured.

"What?"

"Watching your lips. I think that could easily become my second favorite thing to do."

He didn't have to mention his favorite pastime—the innuendo hung there like a living, breathing thing in the close confines of the booth. Just when she thought she was going to scream into the thick, swirling silence, Quinn tried a new tack.

"Have you lived here all your life?"

"Yes. Although I spent the last few years of my marriage in Mill Valley."

He appeared not to have heard the bitterness in her voice that came from all those years of playing the dutiful little suburban housewife for a man who had belatedly decided career women were more stimulating.

"That's not it," he mused aloud, more to himself than to her.

Jessica realized it was useless to argue with this man once he'd made up his mind about something. Oh well, she thought, he'd eventually have to realize they'd never met. Because if there was one thing Jessica knew with an ironclad certainty, it was that this was not the type of man a woman could meet and forget.

Possessing an eidetic memory, Quinn knew he'd met Jessica O'Neill before. The idea was disconcerting, because this was not the type of woman a man could easily forget. Her hair was a gleaming sunlit auburn, laced with strands of dark gold. Her blue eyes, fringed with lush, dark lashes, were beautiful. His gaze moved down her slender nose and came to rest on voluptuously full lips.

"Jessica O'Neill . . . Maybe I'm going by the wrong name. Aren't you Judge Terrance MacLaughlin's daughter?"

"That's right. But I haven't been Jessica MacLaughlin for fifteen years," she protested.

Quinn's lips tightened into a firm line. Then he shook his head and gave her a devastatingly attractive grin. "Don't worry about it, I'll get it eventually," he assured her. "Ready to go?"

While Jessica would have loved to stay until the studiously polite waiter threw her out, she suddenly realized she and Quinn were the only patrons left in the small restaurant. She agreed, smiling an apology to the patient staff clustered in a far corner of the room, obviously waiting to go home to their own families.

"Did you leave your car at the hotel?" Quinn asked as they exited the restaurant.

"I don't have a car."

He looked down at her with interest.

"It's expensive to keep a car in the city," she pointed out somewhat defensively. "Besides, San Francisco is an ideal walking city."

"I agree. But why do I feel that your decision to rely on public transportation goes a little deeper than locating an affordable parking garage?"

"That station wagon seemed to symbolize my entire worth as a wife," Jessica admitted. "I left it back in Marin County with the hot tub, the tennis court and my former spouse."

"And now that you've eschewed suburbia, you feel reborn into a modern career woman of the eighties."

"Precisely." Her tone challenged him to disagree. Something Quinn had no intention of doing.

"My car's back at the hotel," he said instead. "If you don't mind walking off some of those Szechwan prawns, we'll retrieve it and I'll drive you home."

"That's not necessary. I can take a taxi."

"Hey, I may be unfamiliar with the logistics of courting a genie, but the least you can let me do is see you home to your bottle."

"You're crazy."

He grinned down at her. "About you," he agreed.

The warmth in his deep tone and the lambent flame in his eyes caused a shiver to skim up Jessica's spine. She tried to suppress the slight sensation, which did not go unnoticed.

"You're cold. I should have noticed the fog's come in." He immediately slid out of his jacket, holding it out to her. "Put this on."

"I don't need it," she protested.

"Don't be so stubborn," he argued. "Wearing my jacket is not agreeing to a lifetime commitment." His tone was firm, but his eyes were still smiling. "Unless there's an old Irish custom I'm unaware of that states when a man lends his coat to a lovely woman, he's actually proposing marriage."

"Of course there's not." Jessica gave up, accepting the warmth of the superbly cut tuxedo jacket. "Besides, this woman definitely isn't in the market for a husband."

Quinn refrained from answering as he heard the unmistakable clanging bell. "Want to take a cable car back?"

"I'd love it," Jessica agreed, taking his hand as they ran to board the clattering, clanging national monument.

They chose an outer bench and as they made the turn at Grant and California, Jessica slid against Quinn. When she attempted to move away, his arm went around her shoulder, keeping her close. All too soon they reached the hotel.

"Want to stay on and ride for a while?" His green eyes sparked encouragement.

Jessica was feeling amazingly like Rip Van Winkle awakening after a long sleep. She couldn't remember feeling so young, so carefree. She wanted the night to go on forever. She also knew it couldn't.

"I have to get home," she said, her flat tone revealing that it wasn't her first choice.

"I thought you said your mother was with your daughters."

Jessica sighed as she jumped down from the cable car. "She is. But I don't know what she's doing there."

Quinn's arched brow invited elaboration.

"Jill said something about her leaving Dad. I haven't the foggiest idea what's going on, and to be honest, I never should have stayed out this long."

Jessica expected an argument, but Quinn surprised her. "Then we'd better get you home right away," he said, handing his parking stub to the valet. "You seem to have your hands filled with domestic spats these days."

"You know, life would probably be a great deal simpler if Congress simply passed a law abolishing matrimony."

It was impossible to miss the trace of bitterness in her tone, but Quinn was saved from answering by the arrival of his Maserati. Jessica gave him directions to her home and for a time both seemed content to allow the easy silence.

"How long have you been divorced?" he asked, knowing the answer already.

"A little over three years," Jessica said, eyeing him curiously. "Why?"

"Don't you ever consider remarrying?"

Her laugh was short and harsh. "Never."

"Never?"

"I wouldn't get married again for all the tea in China," she professed firmly. "Looking back on it now, I realize that my entire worth as a wife was as cheerleader for my husband. All Brian wanted was an avid and eager audience who'd sit spellbound while he talked about his real estate deals and recited his latest achievements."

"Didn't you have your own goals and aspirations?"

Jessica thought back on Brian's insistence that she drop out of law school. "Of course I did," she responded curtly. "But Brian was always too busy, or too tired after a long day at work to listen to what he considered the petty events of my life."

She shook her head as if to clear it of unhappy memories. "Now, for the first time in my life, I'm doing what I want to do. Not what someone expects me to do."

It wasn't at all what he wanted to hear, but Quinn was undaunted. "What about your daughters?"

Jessica gave him a puzzled glance. "What about them?"

"Don't you want them to have a father?"

She folded her arms across her chest. "They have a father. They spend two weekends a month with Brian and Deirdre, every other Christmas and six weeks every summer. In fact, they probably see more of their father than they did when we were married. Spending time with his family was not one of my former husband's highest priorities."

"So you really did get a civilized divorce?"

"It was extremely civilized," she said dryly. "In that respect it was precisely like my marriage. Utterly predictable and devoid of any honest emotion."

What on earth had possessed her to admit that? To outsiders, the O'Neill marriage had seemed idyllic. For political reasons, Brian had wanted it to appear so, and Jessica had never seen any reason to set the record straight. That had been one of the reasons their divorce had garnered such interest. That and the fact that the handsome candidate for governor had left his wife and three children for another woman.

"Weren't you upset when he . . ."

Quinn's voice trailed off as he realized he'd been about to ask a highly indelicate question. Not that he wasn't curious; he just didn't know if Jessica would be willing to discuss her husband's well-publicized infidelity with him.

"Of course I was," she admitted. A slow, reluctant grin curved her lips. "I broke every dish in the house."

Quinn returned the smile. "Good for you." He reached over and squeezed her hand.

Jessica realized that aside from work, this was the first time in ages she'd been alone with another adult. Enjoying the camaraderie, she allowed her hand to remain in Quinn's larger one the rest of the way home.

"Nice house," he observed, pulling up to the curb outside her quaint Victorian town house.

"It will be. There's still tons of work to do on it, though," Jessica told him. "The first year, while I was in law school, all we could manage was a coat of paint. The next year I had the plumbing replaced. Last year I sprang for a new roof and next month we're having the entire place rewired."

"Sounds as if you've got a lifetime project going."

"I think I do." She grinned. "But it keeps me out of pool halls."

Quinn smiled at the incongruous image. Then, unable to help himself, he leaned toward her, tucking a thick russet curl behind one ear.

"Thank you."

Jessica was more than a little shaken by his suddenly solemn tone. "For what?"

"Rescuing me tonight." Quinn's hand was stroking her cheek, leaving sparks wherever he touched.

"You certainly didn't look like a man in need of rescuing. That blonde was practically eating you alive with her eyes."

Those attractive lines crinkled out from his eyes. "You noticed."

"It was hard to miss," Jessica whispered, struggling to remain indifferent to the fingers lightly spanning her throat. Quinn felt her swallow and knew Jessica was not unaffected by what was happening here.

"It was even harder to get away gracefully. I was wishing for someone—anyone—to save me. And you came. My lovely genie."

Jessica wondered if Quinn could feel the rapid rise in her pulse rate as his husky tone stirred something deep and long forgotten within her.

"You're very fanciful." She laughed unsteadily, backing away both physically and emotionally from the provocative moment.

Stifling a slight sigh, Quinn allowed her to inch toward the passenger door. "I'd better get you in before your mother decides to investigate whether we're necking out here."

His tone was far steadier than his emotions at the moment, and it was only all those years practicing trial law that allowed Quinn to pull off this nonchalant air. What he really wanted to do was pull Jessica into his arms and never let her go.

"That's a good idea," she agreed with matching casualness.

As Quinn opened his door, the dome light came on, flooding the interior of the Maserati with light. The raw desire on Jessica's face was sufficient compensation for tonight, he decided. It was enough to know that at this moment she wanted him as much as he wanted her.

"Are you free for lunch tomorrow?" he asked as he walked her to the front door.

"I've got a lunch date," Jessica stated, refraining from mentioning that it was with Vanessa Parker, the only other woman attorney employed at Bennington, Marston, White and Lowell.

"How about a drink after work?"

"Sorry."

"Another date?" he inquired grittily, not bothering to hide his irritation.

"Something like that."

Jessica knew Quinn was suspecting the worst, but what business of his was it if she wanted to date every man in San Francisco? Deciding it would do him good to discover that not every woman in the city was swooning at his feet, she didn't admit she had to pick up Sara's ballet slippers before the shoe repair shop closed at five-thirty.

"Dinner?"

She had to give him an A for tenacity. "I'm sorry, Quinn, but—"

"I know," he muttered, shoving his hands into his pockets. "You've got another date."

"Not exactly," she found herself admitting.

His expression brightened slightly. "Washing your hair?"

"No."

"Washing your mother's hair?"

She laughed at that one. "No."

"Your daughters'?"

"Close. Sara, my youngest, has a dance recital at the War Memorial Opera House. She's been practicing her pirouettes for weeks. It's like living with a human top."

Quinn laughed. "Well," he stated on an exaggerated sigh, "I suppose I'll have to settle for seeing you in court."

"Speaking of which..." Jessica suddenly realized she'd been so entranced with Quinn's company that she hadn't even insisted he make his client replace Sylvia's Mercedes.

"I know, there's still the little matter of a severed Mercedes."

"It's not a little matter," she pointed out briskly.

"Since California is a community property state, why don't we let them each take a half?"

"That isn't funny!"

"Come on, Jess," Quinn coaxed. "Can't you see the humor in the situation? By the time the two of them are finished, there won't be anything left to divide."

"You may find the entire situation humorous, but I'm not fortunate enough to be a senior partner in one of the city's most prestigious law firms," she retorted. "Your horrible client has put my job in jeopardy, and you'll have to excuse me if I can't see my way clear to laugh about it!"

From the way her voice faltered, Quinn realized Jessica was not as self-confident as she led one to believe. While that could work in his favor, he'd have to proceed cautiously.

"I'll talk to Keith," he assured her, his hands shaping her stiffened shoulders. "I promise he'll be on his best behavior from now on."

"He'd better be," Jessica grumbled. "Because Sylvia is threatening to shoot the minute she sees the whites of his eyes."

"Then the guy's safe."

"What does that mean?"

"You've heard of the three-martini lunch?"

She nodded.

"Keith Thacker is a proponent of the five-martini breakfast. On a good day the whites of his eyes look like a map of the Los Angeles freeway system." Quinn winked, earning a crooked smile from Jessica.

"You're not at all what I expected," she murmured, more to herself than to Quinn as she turned away to unlock her door. She took off his jacket, feeling oddly deprived of its woodsy, masculine scent as she returned it to him. "Thanks for dinner."

"It was my pleasure," he said, nodding his head.

Jessica had to thrust her hands behind her back to keep from reaching up and brushing back that curl that had fallen over his forehead once again.

"Well, good night," she murmured.

"Good night, Jess." He reached out, feathering a light path up her cheek with his knuckles. "Sweet dreams."

Jessica closed her eyes momentarily at the tender touch, half afraid Quinn was intending to kiss her, half terrified he might not.

Not immune to the desire he'd seen in those soft blue eyes before her lush lashes fluttered down, Quinn forced himself to back away from the sensual moment. Jessica was obviously a strong, independent woman, but when it came to relationships, the lady was as skittish as a doe. One false move and she'd take off running.

As much as he wanted to taste those lushly pink lips, he couldn't risk it. Not yet. He ruffled her hair in a friendly, almost fraternal gesture.

"See you in court, counselor," he said in a casual tone.

Jessica's eyes flew open. "In court," she echoed, watching him take the steps two at a time.

She experienced the oddest feeling of sadness as he drove away, and wondered what it was about Quinn Masterson that could make her respond so uncharacteristically. She couldn't remember the last time she'd laughed so freely. Or allowed an evening to pass without phoning home to make certain the girls were in bed on time. It was as if she had been a different person tonight. Jessica glanced up at the gleaming white moon hanging over the city, wondering if there was any truth to the notion that people behaved differently under the influence of a full moon.

The question of her uncharacteristic feelings was a complex one, and Jessica suddenly realized exactly how exhausted she was. It had been a long and tiring day, and if she knew Keith and Sylvia Thacker, tomorrow wasn't going to be one iota easier. She went into the darkened house, unerringly locating the couch, and sank down. Leaning her head back against the cushions, she shut her eyes.

"Jessica?" a voice inquired from the hallway. "Is that you?"

Jessica stifled a groan. "It's me, Mom. I'm sorry I woke you."

"I was awake." The censure in Elizabeth MacLaughlin's tone was unmistakable. "I couldn't sleep until my little girl was back home, safe and sound."

Jessica reined in the temptation to remind her mother that as the mother of three daughters, one a teenager, she was far from infancy. "I'm safe enough," she assured Elizabeth as the older woman entered the living room, tying the sash of her silk robe. "But as for sound . . ." Jessica's voice drifted off as she rubbed the back of her neck.

"You work too hard."

"Please, let's not get into that again. I certainly didn't plan for things to go so wrong today. Speaking of which, what on earth is going on? Jill told me you've left Dad."

Elizabeth MacLaughlin smoothly ignored Jessica's question. "What you need is a cup of tea and something to eat. I'll bet you didn't have dinner, did you?"

"I ate downtown," she hedged, not wanting her mother to know she'd gone to dinner with Quinn Masterson.

"Where?"

Jessica shrugged. "A little Chinese place. I forget the name."

"The food was probably loaded with monosodium glutamate," Elizabeth said with blatant disapproval.

"Probably," Jessica agreed. "That's what makes it taste so good."

Her mother shook her head. "Now you're teasing me. You're as bad as your father."

"Speaking of Dad . . ." Jessica inserted quickly, hoping her mother would explain why after forty-six years of marriage, she'd suddenly shown up on her daughter's doorstep.

"Tell me about the Thackers' latest escapade," Elizabeth said, sidestepping the issue. "Did you see his cartoon in the _Star_ today? He's very talented." Elizabeth's brow furrowed. "You know, your father and I used to be very good friends with Keith's parents. It's too bad he ended up an alcoholic. However, I have to admit I'm not that surprised. Mary spoiled the boy rotten."

Jessica refrained from answering that San Francisco's most controversial political cartoonist had problems that went far deeper than an indulgent mother.

"I'd better be getting to bed," she said, rising from the couch. "I've got a hectic day tomorrow."

"What you need is a husband," Elizabeth advised, not for the first time. "Someone to take care of you and the girls for a change."

Jessica decided not to fall back into the old argument that she was quite capable of taking care of her family all by herself. She was more interested in finding out the reason behind Elizabeth MacLaughlin's recent actions.

"Speaking of husbands—"

"Good night, dear," her mother stated firmly.

Shaking her head in frustration, Jessica bent and kissed the top of her mother's head. The natural auburn hair was still as vibrant as Jessica's, without a hint of gray.

"Good night, Mom." Jessica suddenly wanted nothing more than to fall into bed and sleep around the clock.

But sleep was not that easily found, she discovered much, much later. She couldn't get Quinn Masterson out of her thoughts. It was as if his smiling green eyes and handsome face had been indelibly printed onto her mind's eye. It had been over three years since she'd had a casual evening alone with a man. In the beginning, she'd been hurting too badly to even consider the idea.

Later on, trying to juggle law school with the bringing up of three spirited children precluded anything that remotely resembled a social life. Now, while her life was going a little more smoothly, it was still a simple matter to beg off any invitations from the men she'd meet in the course of her workday. Not many men could remain undaunted by Jessica's ready-made family.

But tonight had been different. There had been such an inevitability to it. If she were a more fanciful person, Jessica might have thought her meeting with Quinn was preordained. But she prided herself on being an extremely practical woman and did not believe in kismet, fate or anything to do with stars, horoscopes or numerology. Or full moons, either, she reminded herself briskly. Those ideas she willingly left to the romantics of the world.

Yet, Jessica considered, lying in bed, her head pillowed by her arms, she'd almost felt romantic tonight. She'd forgotten how nice it was to feel a man's firm hand on her back. Or what a pleasant experience it could be to linger over dinner, sharing conversation that had nothing to do with orthodontist appointments, permission slips for seventh-grade field trips or Girl Scout cookie sales.

It was odd. She'd grown used to all the labels. Divorcée, single head of household, ex-wife, mother, attorney. Any one of those terms could accurately describe Jessica O'Neill. But until this evening, she'd forgotten the most intriguing one of all. Woman.

For a few fleeting wonderful hours Quinn had made Jessica feel like a woman. He'd managed to transport her to a magical realm where she was alive, desirable, utterly fascinating. For that, she was grateful. She'd always remember it as a special evening with a very nice man. Of that Jessica was certain. Just as she was certain it would never happen again.

3

THE SMELL OF BURNING BACON wafted into Jessica's subconscious the following morning and she groaned, pulling the rose-hued comforter over her head. Muffled conversation drifted up the stairs, the steady drone punctuated at intervals by a raised voice or grievous shout.

"Mom! You have got to do something about Mallory and that damn camera of hers."

The insistent tone refused to be ignored and Jessica threw off the comforter, eyeing her daughter standing in the doorway. Smoke practically poured from Jill's ears.

"Don't cuss," Jessica answered automatically. "What has Mallory done now?"

"She invaded my privacy!"

Stifling a sigh, Jessica climbed out of bed, reaching for her robe. "She's been doing that all week and I haven't heard a word of complaint," she pointed out. "In fact, if I recall, you were rehearsing for a starring role last night."

"That was before I knew she was going to hide in the closet and tape my telephone conversations. Mom, she filmed me telling Lori what a hunk Tommy Drew is!"

"Sounds like the end of the world to me," Jessica agreed calmly.

"Mother! This is serious!"

Remembering her own teenage traumas, Jessica forced herself to remain patient. "I'll talk with her," she promised. "After I have a cup of coffee."

"Good." Jill nodded with a vast amount of youthful satisfaction as she left the room and headed back downstairs. "Hey, Mallory," she hollered, "are you ever in trouble now!"

Jessica shook her head, going over to her closet. A list of possible choices was posted on the back of the closet door, and she wryly decided that since Brian had forced her to join the ranks of career women, it had been nice of him to arrange her wardrobe beforehand.

It had been her inherent lack of clothes sense that had provided the impetus for the breakup of their marriage in the first place. Although after the first pain had passed, Jessica was forced to admit the writing had been on the wall for a very long time before Deirdre Hanson had entered the picture.

The entire O'Neill-for-governor campaign staff had unanimously decided that Jessica didn't project the proper image for the wife of an up-and-coming politician. Her jeans and paint-spattered sweatshirts might possess a certain cachet in the artists' communities of North Beach and Sausalito, but they were a definite liability when seeking the yuppie vote. It was the general consensus of opinion that Jessica O'Neill was decidedly lacking in style.

An interior decorator, Elizabeth MacLaughlin was as different from her daughter as night from day, and it was only natural Jessica would turn to her mother for advice. When Elizabeth suggested a visit to The Emporium-Capwell, little did Jessica realize what a difference that shopping trip would make in her life. She was introduced to the store's career dressing coordinator, a tall, striking woman in her thirties, who promised to coordinate her mismatched pieces of clothing into a workable, stylish wardrobe. Since Jessica spent most of her days in Mill Valley, it fell to Brian to stop by the fashionable department store at frequent intervals to take home the chic clothing Deirdre had accumulated.

Now Jessica's closet boasted a treasure trove of Ultrasuede suits, silk blouses, linen blazers and Italian pumps fashioned out of buttery-soft leather. And Deirdre, in turn, had Jessica's husband. Jessica had decided long ago that she'd gotten the better of the trade.

She showered and dressed quickly, then followed the billowing black cloud and the blare of the smoke detector's siren downstairs.

"Mother!" Mallory jumped up from the table. "Would you please explain the First Amendment to Jill? She's threatening to break my camera."

Jessica smiled benignly at her family, going over to pour a cup of coffee. "Good morning. Did everyone sleep well?"

"Mother, did you hear me?"

"Of course I did, dear," she murmured, pulling a pad of paper and a pen from a drawer. "But if you expect a treatise on the First Amendment before I've had my coffee, I'm afraid you're going to be disappointed."

"I told you she wouldn't back you up," Jill said, her hands clenched into tight fists at the hips of her crimson parachute pants.

"She didn't say that," Mallory retorted. "She only said we'd have to wait for a decision until after she had her coffee. So there."

"Mallory O'Neill," Elizabeth stated firmly, "don't stick your tongue out at your sister."

"She's not my sister," Mallory countered. "Gypsies stole my sister from the hospital nursery and left Jill in the bassinet in her place. By the time Mom and Dad discovered the mistake, the Gypsies were long gone and they were stuck."

Jill turned her back, going to the refrigerator to take out a pitcher of orange juice. "You're a riot, Mallory. In fact, you could probably go on the stage with that routine. It's just too bad you've got railroad tracks for teeth."

Knowing her middle daughter's sensitivity about her braces, Jessica prepared herself for the impending storm. When it didn't occur, Elizabeth and Jessica exchanged a long, curious look.

"Jill, you owe your sister an apology," Jessica said sternly.

To her further amazement, Mallory only shrugged. "That's okay," she stated blandly. Then she grinned. "I'm selling outtakes of Jill trying out Gran's mudpack. If the advance orders are any indication, they're going to go like hotcakes all over school." She picked up her camera and escaped the room, a wild-eyed Jill close behind.

Jessica shook her head. "Why did I have three children?"

"Because you didn't want four," Elizabeth offered. "Here, I thought you might enjoy a home-cooked breakfast."

Jessica stared down at the charred strips of bacon and something she vaguely recognized from her youth as scrambled eggs. "You didn't have to go to so much trouble."

Elizabeth smiled with the air of a woman who had never possessed a single insecurity. "It's the least I can do. Especially since I'll be staying here until I get settled."

"About that—"

Jessica's question was cut off as a whirling dervish spun into the room, twirling her way into a chair. "How's that, Mom?" she asked breathlessly.

Jessica grinned at her youngest across the table. "Dynamite. Dame Margot Fonteyn couldn't have done it better."

The freckled face was wreathed in a smile. "Thanks. I'm really nervous about tonight."

"Your mother used to worry, too," Elizabeth said, placing an identical plate of food in front of Sara, who looked at it with suspicion. "With good cause," she murmured under her breath.

Busy scrutinizing the morning meal, Sara missed her grandmother's qualifying statement. "Isn't this the same thing we had for dinner last night?"

"Of course not," Elizabeth scoffed.

"It looks the same."

"Well, it's not."

"It's the same color," Sara persisted with a nine-year-old's tenacity. She sniffed the air, as if noticing the smoke for the first time. "And it's burned."

"It's well done," her grandmother countered, joining them at the table.

Sara pushed the plate away. "Well, I'm not going to eat anything today, anyway. Ballerinas never eat before a performance," she stated, tossing her head regally. Then a frown furrowed her freckled forehead. "Mom, you won't forget to pick up my shoes, will you?"

"It's at the top of the list," Jessica answered, tapping her pencil on the pad.

Sara's grin blossomed. "Thanks, Mom—you're the best." She jumped up from the table.

"Sara, you have to eat something," Jessica insisted, nevertheless understanding her daughter's reluctance to sample the breakfast that had been placed in front of her.

"Don't worry, I'll stop at the deli and pick up a bagel," she promised, blowing a kiss as she executed a grand jeté out the door.

Elizabeth frowned as she watched Sara leave the house. "Your daughters have atrocious eating habits. They only picked at their food last night."

Jessica wondered how such an intelligent woman as her mother had never caught on to the fact that she was a horrendous cook. "They're all at a difficult age," she replied instead, pushing her own food unenthusiastically around the plate. "They think they need to diet."

"I still don't approve," Elizabeth said firmly. "But far be it from me to interfere with the way you rear your children. What are you doing for lunch today?"

"I'm going out," Jessica murmured, writing down her engagement with Vanessa as she answered. It wasn't that she would forget their weekly luncheon; Jessica was an incurable list maker. It always gave her a feeling of accomplishment at the end of the day when she could draw a bold, black line through the final item.

"Why?" she asked, eyeing Elizabeth suspiciously. "What's the matter now?"

"Why should anything be the matter? Can't a mother drop by to have lunch with her daughter without everyone suspecting the worst?"

Jessica sighed. "Don't play coy, Mother. What's up? Is it something to do with Dad?"

"In a way."

Jessica ground her teeth, making mental apologies to the orthodontist who'd spent years correcting her overbite. "Mother, could you simply tell me what you're up to, without making me drag it out of you, bit by agonizing bit?"

"I wanted you to come with me to look at that vacant office down the hall from yours."

"Why?"

"Why do you think? I'm thinking of leasing it."

"Why?" Jessica repeated.

"For my business, of course."

"But you've always worked out of the house," Jessica protested, having grown up surrounded by the bolts of fabric and rolls of wallpaper that were part and parcel of her mother's successful interior design business.

"I don't live there any longer, dear," Elizabeth reminded her patiently. "So, since I had to find a new location, I thought it would be nice if I leased an office close to yours. That way we could have lunch together more often. What do you think?"

Out of a deep-seated sense of parental respect, Jessica refrained from telling her mother exactly what she thought of the scheme.

"Does Dad know what you're up to?"

Elizabeth expelled a frustrated breath as she rose from the table. "Honestly, Jessica," she said stiffly. "Whose side are you on, anyway?"

"It's a little difficult to choose sides when neither of you will tell me what's going on," Jessica pointed out.

Elizabeth busied herself by scraping the uneaten breakfasts into the garbage disposal. "Since your father's retirement, he's become an entirely different man," she answered finally. "He's dictatorial, unbelievably stubborn, and believe it or not, he's behaving like the world's champion male chauvinist."

"But Dad's always been that way."

Elizabeth glanced back at Jessica over her shoulder. "Really?" Her tone displayed honest surprise.

"Really."

"I wonder why I never noticed that before," she said thoughtfully. "Isn't it odd how you can live with a man for years and never see his faults?"

Jessica thought back on her parents' marriage—one she'd always viewed as idyllic. "Mom, don't you love him anymore?"

"Of course I do. But that has nothing to do with it. I simply can't live with the man any longer." With a slight sigh, Elizabeth changed the subject. "What would you like me to fix for dinner?"

"You don't have to cook," Jessica hurried to assure her.

"Nonsense. I want to earn my keep around here."

Jessica's mind went into overdrive as she tried to come up with a way to forestall her mother's culinary efforts. "Why don't we all go out after the recital? I'm sure Sara will be too nervous to eat beforehand. We can make it a celebration."

"All right, dear," her mother agreed cheerily. "That will give me more time to look for office space."

Jessica murmured an agreement, then, eyeing the copper clock on the wall, she jumped up, kissing her mother on the cheek.

"Gotta run," she explained. "I've got exactly two minutes to catch the bus."

With that she raced out the door, arriving at the bus stop just as the doors closed. The driver reopened them with obvious irritation, his mood not improved as Jessica dug through her purse, searching for the proper change. As she finally sank onto a seat at the back of the bus, she said a small, silent prayer that the remainder of her day would go more smoothly.

IF JESSICA NEEDED FURTHER PROOF that the gods were not on her side, the constant stream of emergencies she was forced to deal with once she arrived at her office would have convinced her once and for all. Sylvia Thacker called every ten minutes, wanting to know exactly when her husband would be behind bars.

Another client, a real estate developer suing a local television station for libel, belatedly admitted that there might be "a glimmer of truth" in the reports of several thousand dollars in kickbacks being given to members of the zoning commission, after all. Since the case had been highly publicized, Jessica knew it would be impossible to keep the firm's name out of the papers now that the man was withdrawing his suit.

When called on the carpet for not discovering the truth before filing, she couldn't resist pointing out to George Bennington that he'd been the one to file the damn suit, leaving her to figure out how to prove their case. In turn, the founder of Bennington, Marston, White and Lowell coolly reminded Jessica that she had only been invited to join the firm in the first place as a favor to her father. He, for one, had never approved of women attorneys. They were too emotional, he alleged, his steely gaze indicating that he found Jessica's irritation nothing more than feminine pique.

After that less than successful meeting, she was forced to cancel her lunch date in order to accompany a prominent neurosurgeon across town while he gave a deposition to the IRS concerning his financial interests in several Bahamian banks.

By three-thirty that afternoon, Jessica's head was aching, her stomach was growling, and she'd yet to cross a single thing off her list. When the intercom buzzed, signaling another call that undoubtedly meant more bad news, she felt like throwing the telephone across the room.

"Yes?" she bit out.

"Uh-oh. You're having a bad day." Quinn Masterson's deep voice came across the line, a welcome respite from the constant stream of petty irritations.

"I've had better," she admitted, glancing up at the mirror on the far wall, relieved that her caller couldn't see her.

Her unruly auburn hair, responding to the high humidity in the air, had sprung in a wild tangle of curls. She'd spilled a cup of coffee earlier in the day that had left a large brown splotch on her gray flannel suit. Jessica couldn't help comparing her appearance with that sleek blonde who'd seemed so fascinated with Quinn at the ball last night.

"Would you like some good news?"

"I'd love some," she answered immediately. "Please tell me that Keith Thacker delivered a new Mercedes to his wife today."

"Can't do that," he replied cheerfully. "But I'm prepared to offer a compromise."

"Let's hear it," Jessica agreed on a sigh.

"He'll give her the BMW if she returns his Nautilus exerciser and gives him custody of Maximilian."

"Maximilian?"

"The Lhasa apso," he reminded her with a deep chuckle that had her smiling in spite of herself. "Remember, the little guy that was named stud of the year by the Bay Area Kennel Society?"

"How could I forget?" Jessica answered dryly. "It sounds reasonable to me. Let me call Sylvia and get back to you."

"Fair enough," he agreed amiably. "Want to discuss it over drinks?"

"I'm sorry, but—"

"I know. You've got another date." His tone deepened. "I was hoping you'd changed your mind."

The invitation in his voice was unmistakable and Jessica glanced down at the list she'd made this morning, grateful for an honest excuse to turn him down. She was too tempted to see Quinn again, she admitted to herself. Too drawn to him.

"I can't," she murmured.

There was a slight pause before Quinn answered. "I see. Well, I'm going to be tied up in conferences the rest of the afternoon, but you can leave a message with my secretary when you get an answer from Mrs. Thacker."

"I will," she said softly, unreasonably disappointed by the fact that she'd have no further reason to talk with him today. "Oh, thanks again for dinner last night."

"I enjoyed it," he said simply. "Do you like Indian food? I know a place that serves dynamite curried lamb."

"I don't think so."

"Curry takes some getting used to," he agreed cheerfully. "How about Greek food?"

Jessica shook her head. "It's not that," she said, her tone hesitant.

Quinn wondered why he just didn't hang up and write Jessica O'Neill off as an impossible quest. He was certainly not used to courting rejection, nor was he in the habit of chasing after a woman. But then again, he reminded himself, Jessica was no ordinary woman.

"Why don't I call you later this week?"

It took every ounce of willpower Jessica possessed to refuse that enticing invitation. "I don't think so."

Quinn made an impatient sound. "May I ask a question?"

Jessica swallowed hard and nodded.

"Jessica? Are you still there?"

"I'm still here."

"Good. Are you involved with someone?"

"No," she answered honestly, preparing to tell him that was just the point.

Jessica had no plans to become romantically involved with any man. Her independence had not come easily, and she wasn't willing to give it up for anyone. No matter how warm his green eyes or enticing his smile.

Quinn didn't give her the chance to make her carefully rehearsed speech. "Now that's the best news I've heard all day," he said on a husky chuckle that stirred her even as she fought against it.

"Quinn . . ." Jessica felt obliged to explain.

"Just a minute," he stated in a brusque, businesslike tone, giving Jessica the impression he was no longer alone in his office. His next words confirmed that feeling. "I've got to run. But I'll see you soon, okay?"

"It's not okay at all," she protested. "I'm trying to tell you that I'm too busy for any involvements right now. You're a nice man, and I like you, but—"

"Jessica," he interjected firmly, "I'm already late to my meeting, so we'll have to discuss this at some other time. But believe me, sweetheart, you're going to find the entire experience absolutely painless."

With that he hung up, leaving Jessica to stare at the telephone receiver. What experience? Her reverie was cut short as her intercom buzzed, announcing yet another call.

"Yes, Paula," she said on a sigh, answering her secretary's page.

"Mrs. Thacker on line two." The brisk tone displayed no sign of irritation and as Jessica pushed the button with unnecessary force, she wished she could remain as cool and composed as her efficient secretary.

"Mrs. Thacker," Jessica enthused as she greeted the woman for the hundredth time today, "do I have good news for you!"

JESSICA LEFT THE OFFICE LATE, arriving at the shoe repair store just as the elderly manager was drawing the shade on the door. His expression mirrored the one the bus driver had given her this morning, but Jessica was not about to let it deter her from accomplishing the most important thing on her list.

She smiled sweetly at the man, earning a reluctant smile from him as she complimented him effusively on the marvelous job he'd done replacing the worn sole. Jessica had warned her daughter that a new pair of ballet slippers was in order, but Sara had proven stubbornly superstitious, insisting that she absolutely *had* to have her "lucky shoes."

Fortunately, everyone was dressed and ready to go when Jessica burst in the front door. "Here, Sara," she said, tossing the shopping bag toward her youngest. "I've got to change my clothes."

"We're going to be late," Sara complained, her blue eyes appearing even wider because of her unnaturally pale complexion.

"I'll be down in five minutes," Jessica promised.

"They'll take me off the program," the youngster groaned.

"Three minutes and counting," Jessica called down, flinging pieces of her wrinkled suit onto the stairs as she ran.

She grabbed the first thing she came to, a high-necked, Victorian lace blouse paired with a softly gathered flowered cotton skirt that hit her legs at midcalf. It was one of the few outfits that Deirdre hadn't chosen, and although it had been declared far too whimsical for a candidate's wife, Jessica had fallen in love with the look at first sight.

"Laura Ashley," Elizabeth said as Jessica descended the stairs two at a time.

"Laura Ashley?" Jessica repeated blankly, struggling to pin a cameo at her throat without a mirror. With the way her luck was going today, she'd probably puncture a major artery.

Elizabeth stepped in to help. "The designer," she said on an exasperated breath. "Surely even you have heard of her."

"Afraid not," Jessica admitted. "I just liked it. I didn't know it was designed by anyone famous."

Elizabeth secured the catch, stepping back to eye her daughter judiciously. "Well, the look suits you far better than those tailored things *that woman* put you in."

Jessica stifled a smile. Elizabeth had never forgiven Deirdre for breaking up her daughter's home, despite Jessica's avowal that the divorce had been inevitable. It had put a crimp in Elizabeth's wardrobe for a time, since she'd steadfastly boycotted The Emporium-Capwell. Recently Deirdre had opened a boutique in trendy Cow Hollow, that newly restored area downtown where cash registers rang more briskly than cowbells ever had, allowing Elizabeth to return to her favorite department store.

Jessica turned to her daughters with a smile. "Ready?"

"Ready," they chorused, marching out the door single file. It was times like this, when they were sweet and cooperative, that she remembered why she had wanted a large family.

They were barely settled in the taxi when Mallory managed to destroy the peaceful mood. "It would really be neat if you'd fall into the orchestra pit or something, Sara," she declared casually. "It'd make for some really dramatic film footage."

"I think I'm going to be sick," Sara moaned, turning white as newly driven snow. Her freckles stood out even more vividly against her pallor.

While Sara had performed in recitals before, the cast had always consisted of students. This time, after months of auditions, she had gained a small part dancing with members of the San Francisco Ballet Company.

Giving Mallory a warning glare, Jessica managed an encouraging tone. "Of course you're not," she stated blithely. "Those are simply butterflies. All great performers have them."

"Really?" Sara looked doubtful.

"Really," Jessica insisted. "I read just last week that Alexander Godunov got them before every performance."

"Did they go away?"

Jessica kissed her daughter's clammy forehead. "The minute he began to dance."

"I read the very same article," Elizabeth professed firmly.

Jessica could have kissed her eldest daughter as Jill added her two cents to the fictional account. "I read it, too, Sara. Don't worry, you'll be terrific!"

Breathing a sigh of relief, Jessica decided things might go smoothly tonight, after all. She changed her mind when they took their seats in the theater and she discovered Quinn Masterson seated next to her.

"What are you doing here?"

He grinned, appearing unperturbed by her impolite tone. "Didn't you know? I'm a supporter of the arts." Before she could comment, he looked past her at the avidly interested trio of females.

Elizabeth was already sizing him up as future son-in-law material; the appraising gaze was unmistakable. Jill was staring as if Rick Springfield had suddenly appeared in their midst, and even Mallory looked as if she might consider giving Quinn a starring role in her latest epic.

"Quinn Masterson," he said, holding out his hand. "I believe we've met before, Mrs. MacLaughlin."

"Of course," she agreed with an answering smile. "Several times." Her blue gaze narrowed. "However, I had no idea you and my daughter were acquainted."

"We're very old friends," he stated, ignoring Jessica's intake of breath at his outrageous lie. His gaze slid to Jessica's daughters. "You two are every bit as lovely as your mother. I feel sorry for all the men whose hearts are going to be broken."

Jill and Mallory both appeared to melt on the spot, leaving it up to Jessica to introduce the two girls who had suddenly gone mute. A moment later the orchestra began to warm up, drawing everyone's attention to the stage.

"I remembered where we met," he murmured.

"I told you, Quinn," she insisted, "we haven't met."

"Yes, we have. Tonight brought it all back."

She shook her head, keeping her eyes directed to the stage, waiting for the performance to begin. "You're mistaken."

"I couldn't possibly be mistaken about the worst day of my life."

"Terrific," she grumbled, still refusing to believe him. "It's nice to know I made such a wonderful impression."

"It wasn't you. It was the damn dance class."

Jessica turned her head, eyeing him with renewed curiosity. "Dance class? Don't tell me that you attended Madame Sorenson's Academy of Ballroom Dancing, too?"

"Didn't everyone? At least that's what my grandmother alleged when she dragged me there."

At her questioning expression, Quinn elaborated. "My parents died when a tornado hit our farm that summer and I was sent out here to live with my grandparents."

"I'm sorry."

"It was a rough year," he confessed. "Grandmother was shocked to discover that her only living heir was a wet-behind-the-ears Missouri farm kid without what she referred to as *social graces*." Quinn winced, giving Jessica the feeling that the memories were still slightly painful, years later.

"Anyway," he continued, his tone low, his words intended for her ears only, "she talked Madame Sorenson into taking me into that class, even though I was a head taller and five years older than everyone else."

Jessica tried to recall a tall, handsome boy—a younger version of Quinn Masterson—and came up blank.

"The first class I was paired with a skinny little kid who had flaming red pigtails and a ski-jump nose sprinkled with an amazing array of freckles."

Comprehension suddenly dawned. "I remember you!" Jessica exclaimed, drawing irritated glances from the people sitting around her. She lowered her voice. "You scared me to death, Quinn Masterson. You spent the entire two hours scowling at me and cussed every time I stepped on your foot."

He gave her a lopsided grin. "I probably did," he admitted. "Although you were less than graceful, sweetheart. Next to me, you were the worst dancer in the room."

"I'm left-handed," she said defensively. "As well as left-footed. I have trouble following because everything's backward."

Quinn shrugged. "Hey, Ginger Rogers probably couldn't have followed my clumsy steps. Anyway, that was such a humiliating evening, I went back home and told my grandmother that I refused to ever go back again."

His eyes suddenly gleamed with an unmistakable desire. "However, if I'd known what a beauty that freckle-faced little kid was going to grow up to be, you couldn't have kept me away from that class."

Jessica was saved from answering as the houselights dimmed. She was grateful for the darkness; Quinn wouldn't see the color heating her cheeks at his huskily stated words.

She kept her eyes directed toward the stage, but she was unaware of the dancers as she wondered idly if Quinn had ever learned to dance. She'd certainly seen his picture in the paper enough times, squiring a steady stream of glamorous, sophisticated women to society balls.

"We'll have to try it some night soon," he said, his lips suddenly unnervingly close to her ear.

Every instinct Jessica possessed warned her not to turn her head, but it was as if she were merely a puppet, with Quinn Masterson expertly pulling the strings.

"Try what?" she asked softly, staring at the firm lips only a whisper away from her own.

His broad white teeth flashed in a knowing grin, acknowledging that she was not alone in having these moments of odd, sensual yearning.

"Dancing. We're going to have to give it a whirl and see if either of us has improved."

"Quinn, really, this is impossible," Jessica protested, drawing a chorus of loud shushing sounds from the people seated around them.

She could feel the self-satisfaction practically oozing from him as he patted her cheek and returned his attention to the stage. Jessica didn't dare open her mouth to protest when he took her hand under the cover of darkness, his fingers linking perfectly with hers. Gradually, as the dancers whirled across the stage in the bright costumes and the music swelled, it seemed entirely natural for Quinn's thumb to softly stroke her palm.

Later, in the final scene, when Sara finally pirouetted onto the stage with a group of other young dancers, Jessica's blood ran icy cold with maternal anxiety. It was only when the lights came on again that Jessica realized how tightly she'd been gripping Quinn's hand.

"My God," she murmured, staring at the deep gouges in his skin caused by her fingernails, "why didn't you say something?"

Quinn shrugged. "It was nice to feel needed," he said simply.

Then he turned his attention to Mallory and Jill. "Does anyone else around here feel like a double bacon cheeseburger with fries?" he asked, earning an enthusiastic acceptance from Jessica's daughters, who seemed eager to avoid another evening of their grandmother's cooking.

"There's no way all of us will fit into your car," Jessica pointed out, still unwilling to encourage Quinn's company.

He gave her a slow, patient smile. "I've already thought of that," he assured her. "As we speak, a limousine is circling the block."

He certainly didn't lack self-confidence, Jessica considered, trying to think of another reason that his suggestion was impossible. Before she could come up with one, they were joined by Sara, who came running up the aisle, still dressed in the frothy pink net tutu.

"Mom, look at what someone sent me!"

Her wide eyes, exaggerated by the heavy stage makeup, appeared like two blue saucers in her flushed face. In her hand was a slender crystal bud vase, which held a pair of sweetheart roses and a spray of baby's breath.

"It's from an admirer," she stated proudly.

"An admirer?" Mallory's tone was skeptical.

Sara thrust the card toward her. "See. That's what it says." Her youthful expression grew dreamy. "I've never gotten flowers after a performance before," she said on a sigh. "I feel just like a real prima ballerina."

Jessica had a suspicion exactly who had sent the flowers, but when she caught Quinn's eye over Sara's bright auburn head, his gaze was absolutely guileless.

"How would the prima ballerina like to go get a hamburger?" he asked with a smile Jessica was sure worked wonders on women from eight to eighty.

Sara, however, was imbued with a new importance and was not to be taken lightly. "With fries?"

"Of course."

"And onion rings?"

"Can you imagine a hamburger without onion rings?"

She pinned him with a particularly sagacious gaze. "And a double hot fudge sundae for dessert?"

"With nuts," he agreed.

"Is he with us?" Sara asked her mother.

Giving up, Jessica nodded with resignation. "It appears so."

Her youngest daughter's eyes went from Jessica to Quinn, then back again. "It's about time you brought a man home." She turned to Mallory. "I hope you got my *tour jeté* right before the finale."

Mallory nodded. "Mom wouldn't let me use the flood-light, but I think we got enough illumination from the stage lights."

"Good. It was probably my best one ever. Don't you think so, Gran?"

"It was breathtaking," Elizabeth agreed. "Now why don't you go change so your sisters can go ruin their systems with chemicals? We'll meet you out in the lobby."

She'd obviously read one of the latest pop nutrition books, Jessica decided. Her mother was given to embracing short-lived whims and she could only hope that her worries about food additives, as well as this latest decision concerning her marriage were simply the newest in a long line.

"I want to go out like this," Sara complained. "How will anyone know I'm special if I have to change?"

Jessica's stomach suddenly growled, reminding her that she hadn't eaten all day. She was in no mood to argue. "You can't run around San Francisco in that costume," she said firmly, causing Sara's expression to resemble a depressed blood-hound's.

"However," she added with a smile, "you don't have to wash all that makeup off your face until you go to bed."

Sara's smile could have brightened the entire city with its wattage. Shoving the flowers into Jessica's hands, she raced back down the aisle, disappearing through a curtain.

"A decision worthy of Solomon," Quinn murmured. "Just one more facet in the increasingly complex puzzle of Jessica O'Neill."

Jessica had been following Elizabeth, Jill and Mallory to the lobby, but at Quinn's words, she stopped to look up at him.

"I'm not all that complex."

"Of course you are," he argued lightly, reaching out to gently tug one of her curls. "You're the most aggravating, enticing, incomprehensible woman I've ever met. Just when I think I know what's going on in that gorgeous head of yours, you switch gears and leave me behind."

His green eyes gleamed as they roamed her face. "But I've always been fond of puzzles, Jessica. And you're the most fascinating one I've come across in a long time."

Jessica suddenly felt light-headed, a condition she was determined to ascribe to hunger and not the warm gaze directed her way.

"We'd better catch up with the others. That is, if you were serious about eating with us."

"I've never been more serious in my life." Quinn's tone assured Jessica that they were talking about a lot more than cheeseburgers, and her fingers unconsciously tightened about the crystal stem of the bud vase.

Her heart quickened, making her wonder if Quinn could see its wild beating under the ivory lace of her blouse. Something she recognized as desire thickened her blood, curling its way through her body, red and hot, leaving her trembling in its wake. Not even Brian, with the impetuous lovemaking she'd enjoyed in the early days of their marriage, had made her tremble. Jessica was stunned by her response to Quinn, unable to understand it, unwilling to accept it.

"You'd better let me take this," he said, prying her fingers from the slender stem before she snapped it in half. His smile was gently indulgent. "Don't worry, Jess—" his fingertips brushed a feathery path along her fragile jawline "—I won't push." Then he cupped her chin, lifting her hesitant gaze to his. "But I won't give up, either," he warned, his expression tender, but determined.

Then he winked, his grin boyishly attractive. "Come on, sweetheart," he encouraged, his hand resting lightly on her back as he directed her up the aisle. "We've got a hungry crew to feed."

4

LATER AS THEY ALL SAT around a table at a downtown restaurant, Jessica was forced to give Quinn credit. For a lifelong bachelor, he seemed totally at ease with the disjointed conversation jumping around the table. She had grown so used to her daughters cutting one another off, addressing several varied and dissimilar topics at once, that she had come to accept it as a matter of course. Now, viewing it through Quinn's eyes, Jessica was amazed he was able to keep track of what was going on. He even appeared unperturbed by Mallory's camera whirring away, capturing the evening on videotape.

He answered Elizabeth's questions about a case he'd tried last year before Judge Terrance MacLaughlin, and Jessica was not at all surprised that her mother remembered it as a superb presentation. One did not become a partner in such a prestigious law firm as Quinn's without being an excellent attorney. She also couldn't help noticing how attractive he was, his enthusiasm for his profession brightening his tanned face.

At the same time, he fielded questions from Sara, who was vastly interested in this man who'd suddenly shown up in their midst.

"Are you married?"

"No."

Sara nodded understandingly. "Mom's divorced, too," she offered.

"I've never been married," Quinn responded, correcting Jessica's youngest daughter's mistaken comprehension.

"Why not?" she persisted.

"Sara," Jessica warned, "that's a very personal question and absolutely none of your business."

"I don't mind," Quinn replied. He leaned back in his chair, crossing his arms over his chest. "You see, Sara, when I was in college, I came up with a plan for my life."

"Mom does stuff like that," Mallory interjected. "She's the world's greatest list maker."

Quinn gave Jessica a thoughtful glance, then returned to answering Sara's initial question. "Well, it wasn't that I didn't want a wife and children," he assured his avidly interested audience. "I just didn't think I could concentrate my energies on my career and a family, so I decided that I'd go to law school, join a good firm and work to become a partner by the time I was forty. By then I figured I'd have the time to devote to my personal life."

"How old are you, Quinn?" Jill asked, ignoring the blistering warning glare from her mother.

Quinn's eyes twinkled as he slid a meaningful glance Jessica's way. "I turned forty three weeks ago."

The significance of that statement swirled about them, causing Jessica to grow extremely uncomfortable under the watchful gazes of her mother and daughters. She was distinctly relieved when Sara spoke up, continuing her cross-examination of Quinn with the tenacity of a terrier worrying a particularly succulent bone.

"So you don't have any kids, huh?"

"Not yet." He grinned unrepentently at Jessica, who began fiddling nervously with her silverware.

"Then you probably don't go to many recitals like this," Sara continued to probe.

"This was the first," Quinn agreed cheerfully. "And believe me, I thoroughly enjoyed it. You're quite talented, you know."

Sara bobbed her bright russet head. "I know."

"Are you thinking of making it a career?"

She straightened her slim shoulders. "I *am* going to be a professional ballerina," she said firmly. "I plan on studying for five more years, then I'm going to get an apprenticeship at the San Francisco Ballet Company. Then, before I'm twenty I'll be dancing with the New York City Ballet."

"As a soloist?" he queried, a ghost of a smile hovering at the corner of his lips.

"Of course not," Sara said with youthful disdain. "You don't start out as a soloist. I probably won't get that far until I'm twenty-two or twenty-three."

The smile broke free. "You seem to have your life all planned out."

"Of course."

Elizabeth broke in. "Sara's just like Jessica in that regard. My daughter never begins a day without making a detailed list."

"There's nothing wrong with organization," Jessica snapped, annoyed by the way her mother made her sound like some boring, staid individual. Just because Elizabeth flitted her way through life like a lovely, free-spirited butterfly didn't mean everyone had to follow suit.

Her sharp tone was at odds with the carefree celebratory mood, and five heads swiveled at once to study her curiously.

"I'm going to be a cinematographer," Mallory stated into the uncomfortable lingering silence.

Quinn dragged his attention from Jessica, deciding this was no time to attempt to discern what was bothering her. "I figured as much," he said cheerfully. Then he looked across the table at Jill. "And what about you?" he asked, his gaze taking in her spiky hair and bright, neon apple-green minidress. "Are you going to be a famous rock star? Or an actress?"

Jill shook her head as she slurped the last of her cola making a loud, unmannerly sound. "No. This is just a stage I'm going through," she answered calmly. "I'm going to get married and live in a big house and have lots of children."

Jessica's expression could have been carved in granite. "I think it's time we went home," she announced, pushing her chair back from the table and standing up abruptly. "Tomorrow's a school day."

A chorus of dissent echoed around the table. "I haven't finished my sundae," Sara complained.

"Tough," Jessica retorted. "You should have spent more time eating and less time talking." Her icy gaze rose to Quinn. "Thank you very much, but we have to be going."

"Fine. I'll drive you."

"We can get a taxi."

Quinn's smile didn't waver, but his tone was firm. "I think we exhausted that suggestion last night, Jess. I don't invite people out to dinner, then send them home in a taxi."

Jessica felt as if she were being examined under a microscope as four pairs of female eyes suddenly riveted on her.

"You went out to dinner with Quinn last night?" Mallory asked incredulously.

"In that horrid old running suit?" Jill tacked on, her youthful expression displaying what she thought of her mother's casual apparel.

"That explains it," Elizabeth murmured thoughtfully.

Sara simply stared.

Jessica's eyes shot daggers at Quinn, who appeared totally unperturbed by the sudden interest in their relationship.

"Come on, girls," he said, his grin breaking free. "We'd better get you home before your mother lays down the law and grounds us all."

That earned a laugh Jessica refused to acknowledge as she marched out of the restaurant, head held high, her back as rigid as if someone had dropped a rod of steel down her lacy blouse.

If she thought she was going to get away without inviting Quinn in, Jessica was sadly mistaken. As the limousine pulled up in front of the house, she was outnumbered four to one, and her irritation rose to new heights as Quinn cheerfully complied with the majority.

Sara insisted on showing him her scrapbook, and Mallory proudly displayed the certificate won for a short animated film she'd made using space creatures fashioned from modeling clay. Jill, not to be outdone, treated him to a performance of her lipsyncing the latest rock hit.

Finally the three girls had been convinced it was well past their bedtime, and as the adults drank espresso in the living room, only the giggles drifting down the stairs revealed the level of excitement the unusual evening had created.

Jessica was annoyed, but not particularly surprised, when Elizabeth used the opportunity to do a little motherly detective work.

"My husband has always spoken very highly of you, Quinn," she said with a smile. "But I didn't realize you and my daughter were acquainted."

"We're old friends." Quinn's deep voice invested the outrageous statement with a masculine intimacy, causing Jessica to glare at him.

Elizabeth's eyes gleamed with interest, and Jessica could practically see the wheels turning inside her mother's head.

"We're simply business acquaintances," Jessica corrected firmly. "Quinn is representing Keith in the Thackers' divorce case."

Elizabeth had deftly manuevered the seating arrangements so that she had possession of the only chair in the small, intimate parlor, forcing Jessica to share the love seat with Quinn. At her prickly tone, he put his arm around her shoulder and grinned wickedly.

"Don't forget that memorable evening we spent dancing, Jessie."

Elizabeth suddenly popped up, a brilliant smile on her face. "I'm so exhausted," she claimed, her hand covering her mouth to stifle a yawn Jessica suspected was feigned. Her mother had always been a night owl. "I think I'll head up to bed now. Good night, Jessica. Quinn. It was a pleasure seeing you again."

Quinn's eyes danced with amusement at Elizabeth's less than subtle matchmaking. He rose immediately from the couch. "The pleasure was all mine, Mrs. MacLaughlin," he stated. While his words were directed at her mother, his eyes remained on Jessica.

With a throaty chuckle, Elizabeth made herself scarce, leaving Jessica and Quinn alone in the dimly lit room.

Jessica jumped up and turned on him, her hands on her hips. "Why did you do that?"

He arched a gold eyebrow. "Do what?"

"Make my mother think there's something going on between us."

"Isn't there?"

"No." Jessica held her breath, irrationally waiting for a bolt of lightning to strike her down for telling such a blatant lie. She couldn't remember either of them moving, yet a moment later she was standing in the circle of his arms.

"Jessie," he murmured, "didn't your mother ever teach you it's not nice to tell a lie?"

She couldn't think with those warm green eyes moving so slowly over her face. She stared down at the floor.

"Jess." It was only her name, but his husky voice made it a caress. And a command. She slowly lifted her eyes, shaken as she reluctantly met his desirous gaze.

He reached down, taking one of her hands in his, uncurling the fingers from the tight, nervous fist she'd made. Her fingernails had left little gouges in her palm and as he stroked her skin, Jessica could only stare, entranced by the sensual movement of his dark fingertips. When those devastating fingers curled lightly around her wrist, Jessica knew he could feel her pulse racing.

"Do you know the last time I held hands with a girl while her mother was upstairs in bed?" Quinn's tone was conversational, but his eyes were handing her an increasingly sensual message.

"No," she managed, her voice as shaky as her body.

"Neither do I," he admitted with a crooked grin. "But it's been a very long time."

He'd laced their fingers together, bringing her hand to his chest, allowing her to feel his own erratic heartbeat. His eyes were still focused on hers, and Jessica felt as if she was drowning in pools of molten emeralds. Every nerve ending in her body was alive, reaching for his touch.

"Once we settle the Thackers' problems, perhaps we should do a little matchmaking of our own," he suggested. "See if we can do anything to get your parents back together. It would be a shame to stand by and watch a marriage of that long a duration go down the drain."

"My parents are pretty stubborn," Jessica said. "I'm not certain how they'd take to any outside interference." She hesitated. "I'm sorry she behaved that way."

Jessica could feel the rise and fall of his chest under her hand and had a sudden urge to touch his skin, to see if he was beginning to burn with the same intensity that had her body glowing with a lambent heat. She stifled a gasp as he lifted her hand to his lips, pressing a kiss against her wrist, causing her pulse to leap in response.

"That's okay—it was rather endearing. Besides, I think she had a great idea." Quinn breathed in the fragrance of her skin, needing to know if she tasted as sweet. His tongue teased the inside of her wrist.

"Idea?" Jessica's free hand moved up to his shoulder, to support herself against the desire sweeping through her.

"She's expecting me to kiss you good-night."

"I don't think that's a very good idea," she protested weakly. "Besides, you let her think we were romantically involved. 'Very old friends,' you said."

"I *have* known you since you were eight."

"Not since," she countered. "Except for those two hours, we only met yesterday."

"Isn't there an old Chinese proverb that states once you've broken a man's toes, he's yours for life?"

Jessica's heart pounded in her throat. "Not that I've heard."

"Then you obviously haven't been spending enough time in Chinatown," Quinn said with a smile. "I'm certain I heard it only last week." His eyes darkened to a deep, swirling sea, enveloping her in his gaze. "I don't think you should disregard your mother's wishes, Jessica. She has enough problems right now without worrying about a willful daughter."

Jessica watched, transfixed, as his head lowered, his lips approaching hers with sensual intent. *Too fast*, she told herself, even as her own lips parted. *This is happening too fast*.

She pressed her hands against his chest. "No," she whispered, knowing that her eyes were giving him an entirely different answer.

Quinn was unmoved by her weak protest. "Don't fight it, Jessie," he murmured, his lips altering their course, moving along her jaw. As he put his hand on her cheek, coaxing her mouth toward his, Jessica turned her head away in sudden panic.

"I said no, Quinn!" She would have moved away, to safer territory, but his hands were on her shoulders.

"Why not?" The words came out harsher than he intended. But he'd never met a woman capable of making him feel this way, and it was all he could do not to drag her by that long auburn hair to bed right now. Caveman tactics, he considered bleakly, knowing that primitive method would never work with Jessica O'Neill. But damn, how he wanted her!

His angry tone only served to fuel her irritation. Jessica felt her temper rising, but reminded herself that if she lost it, she would give Quinn even more of an advantage than he possessed at the moment.

"I don't think I owe you an explanation," she stated coolly, backing out of his arms.

Quinn bit down a frustrated response, allowing her to move away. "Perhaps you don't owe me one," he admitted. "But it would be nice to know why you suddenly changed your mind. Face it, Jess—a minute ago you wanted me as much as I wanted you."

She tossed back her head. "Even if that were the case, which it's not," she quickly added as she saw the victorious flash in his eyes, "I'm not in the market for an affair, Quinn."

"Scared?" he taunted lightly.

Quinn knew he hadn't misread those soft gazes she kept giving him; he knew Jessica had experienced the same elemental jolt he had when they'd first seen each other last night at the Fairmont. So why did she insist on playing these ridiculous games?

She turned her back, wrapping her arms around herself, as if in self-protection. "That's ridiculous," she said softly, her slight trembling giving her away.

Quinn shoved his hands into his pockets to keep from reaching out and touching her. She *was* frightened, he realized suddenly.

"Is this the same Jessica O'Neill who put her life back together all by herself and who prides herself on her independence? Is this the same woman who has gained the reputation of an *iron lady* around the municipal courthouse this past year?"

She looked back over her shoulder. "You're making that up."

"No, I'm not. In fact, that's one of the more charitable descriptions, if you want to know the truth. You've got a reputation for being a loner, Jess. A woman with ice water for blood and a stone-cold heart."

She was not going to admit how that uncomplimentary description stung. "Why is it that no one questions a man if he chooses not to marry, but if a woman values her freedom, there's something wrong with her?"

"Perhaps it's because you wear your bitterness like a chip on that lovely shoulder," he suggested softly, coming over to stand behind her. "I like this blouse," he murmured. "You look different tonight. Softer." His palms shaped her shoulders, warming her skin under the fragile ivory lace.

"I don't want to look soft," she argued. "I don't want to *be* soft."

Despite her words, Jessica didn't resist as he turned her slowly in his arms. His green eyes as they studied her thoughtfully, were gently censorious.

"I know you've been hurt, Jess," he said quietly. "But don't let your feelings ruin your daughters' chances for happiness."

Jessica knew immediately which particular daughter Quinn was referring to. "Jill," she muttered, shaking her head sadly.

"Jill," he agreed. "She's got a lot of love to give. Don't teach her to bottle it all up, just because you've found that's the safest way to deal with life."

Jessica shook her head, her distress eloquent in her blue eyes. "You don't understand," she whispered. "I was just like Jill at her age. I don't want her to be hurt."

"Of course you don't," he said, his palms rubbing lightly on her back. "But just because Jill wants a family doesn't mean she's going to be hurt. Fifty percent of marriages *don't* break up."

"And fifty percent do," she reminded him.

"Ah, sweetheart, I never would have figured you for a woman who looks at the glass and sees it half-empty," he chided.

She didn't used to be, Jessica admitted secretly. There was a time when she could have been described as an eternal optimist, always expecting the best from life. But she'd learned the hard way what happens to women who wear blinders.

When she didn't answer, Quinn heaved a deep sigh. "I'd better be going."

She slowly lifted her head, trying to remain unaffected by the lingering desire in his eyes. "Thank you for dinner," she murmured. "It was you who sent Sara the flowers, wasn't it?"

He managed a crooked grin. "Guilty as charged, counselor."

Jessica tried to smile and failed miserably. "It was a very nice thing to do. And I'm sorry if I gave you the wrong impression about..." Her voice failed her momentarily. "You know."

He shrugged. "There'll be another time."

"No, there won't."

Quinn surprised her by smiling, a slow, devastating smile. "Don't bet the farm on that, sweetheart," he warned softly, brushing his knuckles against her cheek. The dazzling smile didn't quite reach his strangely hard green eyes. "Because you'd lose." With that he was gone, leaving Jessica to stare after him.

JESSICA REFUSED TO ANSWER any questions about Quinn the next morning, her stern tone assuring everyone that she was in no mood to discuss her personal life. Even Sara remained silent, although her steady blue gaze was unnervingly knowing for a nine-year-old. Although Sara was the youngest, in some ways she was far more mature than her sisters. Jessica had often thought the child had mistakenly been born with an adult mind.

Jessica managed to reschedule her lunch with Vanessa and after a noneventful morning's work was seated in a white wicker gazebo, in a veritable arboretum, surrounded by blooming plants and live banana palms. The soothing sound of splashing fountains could be heard over the murmurs of the luncheon crowd.

"So," Vanessa said, eyeing Jessica over the rim of her glass, "I hear you and Quinn Masterson are an item."

Jessica slowly lowered her menu, staring across the table at the other woman. They weren't particularly close, but being the only two women working in the decidedly male bastion of Bennington, Marston, White and Lowell had created a certain bond. Lunch discussions, however, seldom included personal topics.

"Where on earth did you hear that?"

"I was at a party last night and Pamela Stuart was sulking because you'd managed to spirit San Francisco's most eligible bachelor away from the Arts' Ball."

"Pamela Stuart?" Jessica's brow furrowed as she tried to place the woman.

"You know," Vanessa said, "Fletcher Stuart's wife."

Jessica knew Fletcher Stuart was one of the city's most successful real estate developers, on a par with her own former husband. She struggled for a mental image of his wife.

"Tall, willowy, blond," Vanessa added, to help out.

Jessica suddenly remembered the sleek woman whose hand had been resting so possessively on Quinn's arm. A jolt of something dangerously akin to jealousy forked through her and it was all she could do to keep a placid, inscrutable expression on her face.

"Are they still married?" she asked with far more aplomb than she was feeling at the moment.

The waiter chose that inopportune time to arrive to take their order, and Jessica was forced to wait for an answer. "Well?" she asked once they were alone again.

Vanessa was crunching on a stalk of celery from her Bloody Mary. "Well, what?"

"Are Pamela and Fletcher Stuart still married?"

Her friend's brown eyes narrowed. "So there is something going on between you two?" Her tone displayed her incredulity. "I figured it was just party gossip. Or a case of mistaken identity. I mean, let's face it, kiddo, you're not really in the same league with Quinn Masterson."

"What exactly do you mean by that?" Jessica asked frostily.

"Hey," Vanessa said quickly, "I didn't mean to hurt your feelings, Jessica. It's just that you don't even date, and Quinn, well..."

"I know," Jessica muttered. "Quinn Masterson has elevated the dating game to Olympian heights."

"The man does have quite a reputation," Vanessa stated cautiously. "I don't think he's ever shown up two nights in a row with the same woman."

"So why was Pamela Stuart making such a big deal about it?" Jessica asked, wondering how the idea of Quinn and all his women could hurt this way. "And you never answered my question. Is she still married?"

"She's married, but to my knowledge that has never slowed her down. As for her relationship with Quinn, I think she has her sights set on him for husband number three. At least she was dropping plenty of hints that the golf-ball-size aquamarine ring she was sporting was an engagement gift from the man."

Jessica suddenly realized she was tearing her paper napkin to shreds and lowered her hands to her lap. "Look, I don't want to talk about him, okay? I did meet with him the night of the Arts' Ball, but only to insist that he control the behavior of one of his clients."

"You're on opposite sides of a case?"

"Yes. And that's all it is."

"Wow," Vanessa murmured, taking a sip of her drink. "If there's one thing more dangerous than getting involved personally with that man, it's probably going up against him professionally."

Her dark eyes surveyed Jessica with renewed interest. "How on earth did you get anything that important? Usually one of the partners handle things in Masterson's league."

Jessica shrugged. "It's not that big a case. It's a divorce. I'm representing Sylvia Thacker."

At that Vanessa laughed. "Now I understand. That woman is an absolute menace and her husband's even worse. As long as her grandfather's estate represents one of Bennington, Marston, White and Lowell's major accounts, none of the guys on the top floor will touch that divorce with a ten-foot pole." She shook her head. "I don't envy you," she said cheerily, before turning her attention to the waiter who'd arrived with their lunch.

Try as she might, Jessica could not get the vision of Quinn and Pamela Stuart out of her mind. It was ridiculous to feel this jealous about a man she had no intention of getting involved with, she knew. She told herself that over and over again as the day wore on, but her heart seemed to have a mind of its own as it steadfastly refused to listen to her head.

When her secretary announced a call from her mother, Jessica stifled a sigh, hoping Elizabeth wasn't going to start in again on her incessant matchmaking.

"Hi. How's the hunt for an office going?" She hoped that starting the conversation out with her mother's life would forestall any mention of Quinn's name.

"Fine, I suppose." Her mother sounded less enthusiastic than she had yesterday. "Although I'll admit I've been having second thoughts about taking space in some impersonal office building."

Hallelujah, Jessica sang out inwardly. Elizabeth was ready to return home. "Oh?" she inquired with feigned casualness.

"I've been thinking about joining the peace corps." Elizabeth dropped her latest bombshell casually.

"Peace corps? At your age?"

She could practically see her mother's spine stiffen. "Lillian Carter was older than I am when she joined."

Deciding that her mother would definitely not appreciate her only daughter pointing out there was a vast difference in the need for nurses and the need for interior decorators in the peace corps, Jessica remained silent.

"What do you think about Alaska?" Elizabeth asked suddenly.

"I don't think the peace corps works in the United States, Mom," Jessica answered, picturing an igloo with Levolor blinds and art deco posters on the ice-block walls.

"Not for me, I was thinking about Africa.... Your father's the one talking about moving to Alaska. Can you imagine the old fool?"

"Alaska? Dad? Why?"

"He's bought a gold mine. Honestly, Jessica, can you picture your father as a prospector?"

Jessica could picture that about as well as she could her mother off in the African bush decorating huts.

"Do you want me to talk to him?" she asked.

"Don't waste your time," Elizabeth snapped. "There's no reasoning with the man lately. Well, if he thinks he's the only one who can have an adventure, he's going to find himself sadly mistaken."

That explained the peace corps notion, Jessica realized, wondering if her parents were going through some sort of delayed adolescence. They'd always been so stable—the rocks that had formed the foundation of the MacLaughlin family. She sighed. Maybe some substance had been dumped into San Francisco's water system, causing all the city's inhabitants to behave totally out of character. The way she'd been acting with Quinn certainly hadn't been normal.

That thought brought to mind Pamela Stuart and her alleged engagement ring. "Look, Mom," Jessica said swiftly, "I've got a call on the other line, but I'll be home for dinner."

"Fine, dear," Elizabeth answered cheerfully. "And don't worry about cooking. I've got everything under control."

Envisioning the mutiny the girls were going to stage if Jessica couldn't figure out some way to keep her mother out of the kitchen, she closed her eyes wearily. "I've got to hang up now," she said. "Oh, and Mom?"

"Yes, dear?"

"Please don't do anything rash until I get home and we can talk about it."

"Honestly, Jessica," Elizabeth huffed with very real indignation. "I don't know where you get these crazy ideas. Sometimes I think you must take after your father. Of course I won't do anything rash. I'm the sensible one in the family, after all."

Jessica shook her head, smiling as she hung up the phone. Her parents were driving her crazy, but she loved them both and only hoped they could work out their difficulties.

Moments later the intercom buzzed again. "Mr. Masterson on line one," Paula's disembodied voice announced.

Jessica fought down the flush of pleasure, reminding herself that to get involved with a man who in earlier times could only be described as a *rake* would be pure folly.

"Hello," she said stiffly. "What can I do for you?"

His answering chuckle was low and deep. "Ah, Jess," he teased. "You should know better than to give me a straight line like that."

His intimate tones caused a warmth to begin deep in her middle regions, spiraling outward until she could feel the tips of her fingers tingling. Her toes literally curled in her tan pumps.

"I assume you're calling to discuss Mr. Thacker," she said briskly, fighting down the unwelcome surge of desire that threatened to be her undoing.

"So it's going to be strictly business where you and I are concerned?"

Jessica tried to read an undertone of regret in Quinn's deep voice, but failed. "I've already told you that," she pointed out briskly. "Several times, in fact."

"That's right, you have," he agreed amiably. "Mr. Thacker extends his appreciation to Mrs. Thacker for having Maximilian delivered so promptly."

"I'm pleased that he's pleased," Jessica murmured, secretly admitting it had come as a surprise when Sylvia had agreed without a word of complaint to her husband's latest proposal.

"Oh, he's not exactly pleased," Quinn added casually. "In fact, I'm giving official notice that he intends to bring a civil suit against Mrs. Thacker for the destruction of private property."

"What?" Jessica's voice rose at least an octave.

As she dragged a hand wearily across her eyes, Jessica reminded herself that she was the one who'd insisted on keeping things on a professional level. Quinn's tone was silky smooth, but as dangerously sharp as a well-honed stiletto, and she suddenly understood Vanessa's comment at lunch concerning his ruthless reputation as an adversary.

"She shaved him, Jess. Right down to the skin."

"Oh, no," Jessica groaned. "She didn't?"

It was a rhetorical question and Quinn didn't bother to answer. "As we speak, Maximilian looks more like a very fat rat than the city's most valuable stud," he informed her.

"I'm sorry."

He surprised her by chuckling, his cold attitude dissolving as quickly as it had appeared. "You probably will be," he agreed cheerfully. "I advised the guy against retaliation, but if you'll take a little professional advice, counselor, I'd warn Mrs. Thacker to take a long vacation out of town."

"I'll talk to her," Jessica said flatly.

"You do that," Quinn replied. "And Jess?"

Here it comes, she thought, a ripple of exhilaration skimming up her spine. *He's going to ask me out and I'm not going to be able to refuse.*

"Yes?" she asked, unable to keep the expectation from her tone.

"See you in court," he said, leaving her feeling slightly annoyed as he hung up.

"The least he could have done was tell me to have a nice day," she muttered as she placed a call to Sylvia Thacker, vowing that this time she wouldn't allow herself to be intimidated by the woman's veiled threats.

It was Sylvia's fault Jessica was mixed up with Quinn Masterson in the first place, and if the Thackers couldn't get their act together, Jessica was simply going to remove herself from the case. She refused to admit that her irritation had anything to do with Quinn's sudden dismissive attitude.

5

IF JESSICA THOUGHT she'd experienced the worst her day could offer, she was in for a surprise as things went from bleak to miserable. Sylvia Thacker showed no remorse about her act of vandalism, stating briskly that a BMW was no fair trade for a Mercedes.

"Then why did you agree to accept your husband's offer in the first place?" Jessica asked wearily.

"Because, my dear, a BMW is still a far sight better than public transportation. Besides—" the woman chuckled wickedly "—I couldn't resist driving Keith's blood pressure up. I only wish I could have been there to see his face when Max was delivered."

Privately Jessica considered that Sylvia's absence from the scene was probably the only reason Keith Thacker wasn't in jail at this very minute, charged with murder.

"He has every intention of suing you," she felt obliged to point out.

"Let him." The woman's voice held a careless shrug. "And we'll sue for the Mercedes, of course."

"Of course," Jessica agreed faintly, mentally ringing up the costs of the continual charges and countercharges made by the Thackers.

While both law firms' coffers were growing the longer the couple fought their marriage out to the bitter end, she hated to consider the way she and Quinn were going to be tying up the already crowded court calendar.

"I've got to go," Sylvia said suddenly. "Keith just drove up."

"Mrs. Thacker, you wouldn't . . ." Jessica left the sentence unfinished, afraid to remind Sylvia Thacker of her earlier threat. Perhaps the woman didn't even own a gun, Jessica considered hopefully.

"Don't worry about a thing, Mrs. O'Neill," her client assured her. "I have everything under control."

As the dial tone echoed in her ear, Jessica could only hope so. She debated phoning the police, then decided that she was probably only borrowing trouble.

She had returned to preparing a brief for an environmental group attempting to gain funds from the EPA Superfund when her intercom buzzed again. Experiencing a fleeting wish for the good old days before telephones, Jessica answered the page.

"Yes? And if you tell me it's Sylvia Thacker, I'm going to slit my wrists."

Paula laughed. "No, it's the judge. You'd better talk to him before he explodes."

Jessica groaned. "Is he that upset?"

"The usually unflappable Judge MacLaughlin could give Mount St. Helen's a run for its money right now," she stated. "What on earth is happening in your family, Jessica? You've gotten more phone calls in the past three days than you have in the past year."

"I don't know," she said on a deep sigh, casting a quick glance at her watch. "Look, I've got a meeting with Mr. Bennington in two and a half minutes. Will you do me a favor and tell Dad that I'll get back to him as soon as possible?"

"Sure. But if you look to the north and see smoke billowing into the sky, don't say I didn't warn you."

Jessica rubbed her fingertips against her temples, gathering strength for the upcoming meeting with the head of the firm. It was her monthly review, a procedure suffered by all first-year attorneys, and though she never found it the least bit enjoyable, she was thankful she no longer broke out in hives when summoned to the executive offices.

Compared to some of the others Jessica had suffered through, this month's review was relatively painless. As she returned to her office, Paula's grave face displayed her concern. The secretary's worried expression broke into a congratulatory grin as Jessica gave her a thumbs-up sign.

"Your father called three more times," she said pointedly, single-handedly managing to burst Jessica's little bubble of pleasure.

Realizing she couldn't keep avoiding the issue, Jessica assured Paula that she'd take care of it immediately. She went into her office and dialed the MacLaughlin residence.

"That better be you, Jessie MacLaughlin O'Neill," her father said abruptly.

"It's me," she acknowledged. "What's up?"

"What's up?" Her father's deep voice vibrated with incredulity. "What's up?" he repeated. "I expected you to tell me. Do you know what fool stunt your mother has come up with now?"

"The peace corps?"

"So you do know."

He jumped on Jessica's words instantly, reminding her of Judge Terrance MacLaughlin's forceful presence on the bench. He'd been strong and tough, but fair, she conceded. She could only hope his sense of fair play extended to his own wife.

"Well, after all, Dad, you're taking off to Alaska to work that gold mine you bought. Surely you can't deny Mom a little adventure of her own."

"Leased," he corrected gruffly.

"Leased?"

"You don't *buy* a gold mine, Jessica. You lease it from the government."

"Lease, buy, what's the difference? You're heading off to Alaska, what do you expect Mom to do? Stay home and knit you some warm clothes for prospecting?"

"She could be more supportive," he grumbled.

"So could you," Jessica risked pointing out.

"You think I should endorse this peace corps thing?" Jessica could practically see her father's silvery brows climbing his wide forehead.

"Did you invite her to Alaska?"

"Why the hell should I do that? If she can't stand to live with me in that huge mausoleum of a house she's always redecorating, how long do you think we'd survive together in a prospector's shack?"

Try as she might, Jessica couldn't see either of her parents living happily in such circumstances. "Dad, why don't you at least ask her?"

"And give her the opportunity to turn me down?"

"Would that be so bad?"

"The man is supposed to be the head of the family, Jessica. It's time Elizabeth realized that."

Jessica was rapidly reaching the end of her patience. "If you don't do something soon, Dad," she told him briskly, "there won't be any family for you to be the head of."

She heard his spluttered protests as she firmly replaced the receiver.

Jessica was more than a little relieved when her excruciatingly long workday came to an end. Despite a continual dosage of aspirin all day, she had a throbbing headache and was feeling ill-tempered and out of sorts. It didn't take a Rhodes Scholar to pinpoint the cause of her discomfort. She'd been feeling rotten ever since Vanessa had told her about Quinn and Pamela Stuart at lunch. If Jessica was distressed by the idea of Quinn involved with another woman, especially a married one at that, she was aghast at how much she cared.

Deciding it would be unfair to submit her family to her bad mood, she chose to walk home, using the time to calm down and dismiss the handsome attorney from her mind once and for all.

She tried strolling through a few art galleries, pretending interest in the collections of paintings and etchings. But when Quinn Masterson's handsome features appeared to be painted on every canvas, printed on every lithograph, Jessica gave up that idea, opting instead for the peaceful respite of Golden Gate Park.

In a city renowned for its economy of space, the park was a vast oasis of open air, the once-desolate wasteland of shifting sand dunes having been transformed into a magnificent, yet seemingly natural, park. Strolling past the manicured lawns and pristine flower beds, Jessica settled down on a bench outside the Conservatory of Flowers, the park's Victorian gem. She breathed in the fresh scent of spring, the sweet perfume of the brilliant blossoms, the heady scent of newly mown grass and slowly began to relax.

With her usual careful, methodical way of tackling a problem, Jessica considered her reaction to Quinn, even conceding that she was undeniably attracted to him. What woman wouldn't be? He was handsome, successful, and although she hated to admit it, his reputation did give him a certain aura that would appeal to many women. Rhett Butler had been a rake, too, and he certainly hadn't fared too badly.

Jessica had to acknowledge that so far Quinn had been a complete gentleman. And he'd certainly managed to charm both her mother and her daughters. She shook her head, wondering at the appeal of a man who had three generations of women responding to his magnetism.

"It's nothing but a silly, schoolgirl crush," she told herself firmly as the setting sun turned the windows of the pyramid shaped Transamerica building to a gleaming bronze. "That's all."

Jessica rose, and leaving the park, headed for home. "Well, maybe it's a little bit more than that," she admitted under her breath, unaware she was talking out loud. "It's also physical. But that's all. Simply sex."

"Hey, lady," a teenage boy drawled from a nearby bench, "that ain't all bad."

Lowering her head to hide her unwilling blush, Jessica walked a little faster, inwardly damning Quinn for this latest display of atypical behavior. She never talked to herself. Certainly never in public!

As she lifted her gaze once more, Jessica's breath suddenly caught in her throat. A tall man was walking a few feet in front of her, his golden hair gleaming with sun-gilt strands in the last light of day. He had broad shoulders, lean hips and the long legs clad in gray flannel slacks were achingly familiar. She was trying to decide whether to say anything when he snapped his fingers, as if he'd just remembered something, and turned around.

Jessica's heart crashed to the sidewalk underfoot as she realized the man's eyes were hazel, not green, and his lips were fringed by a thin mustache. His features were not unattractive, but neither did they cause her pulse to race. As the stranger passed, headed back in the opposite direction, he caught a glimpse of her disappointed face and frowned slightly, as if wondering what he'd done to cause her displeasure. Then he was gone and Jessica was left with the unhappy realization that somehow, when she hadn't been looking, Quinn Masterson had laid claim to her heart.

ELIZABETH MET JESSICA at the door of her town house. "Your father called me this afternoon."

"That's nice," Jessica replied blandly.

"Nice? How can you say that, Jessica O'Neill, after the way you betrayed me. Your own mother!"

Jessica sighed, kicking off her shoes. She should have known better than to walk home wearing a pair of new pumps. She'd be lucky not to get a blister.

"I didn't betray you," she protested, hanging her spring jacket on the brass coatrack.

"Oh, no? I suppose you didn't insist that your father take me to that godforsaken wilderness with him? Honestly, Jessica, if you want me out of your house, just say so. You don't have to ship me off to Alaska like some white slaver!"

"I didn't insist, I suggested," Jessica corrected, trying not to smile at her mother's imaginative description.

"Insist, suggested, what's the difference? The fact remains that you told your father I needed someone to look out for me. So he generously offered his services. The old goat. I know exactly what services he had in mind, too!"

"Mother, you're being unreasonable," Jessica remonstrated, making her way to the back of the narrow house to the kitchen.

Elizabeth was on her heels. "*I'm* being unreasonable? What about your father? Do you know I've read they go in for wife-swapping up there? He probably just wants me along so he'll have someone to hand over to his male guests!" Elizabeth's voice trembled with righteous indignation.

Jessica opened the refrigerator, taking out a half-empty bottle of white wine. "Want some?" she offered.

"Not now," her mother said firmly. "I want to get this settled once and for all, Jessica."

Jessica shrugged, taking down a glass and filling it to within an inch of the top with the crisp white Chablis. "Look Mother, I've had a rough day and I don't need to come home to this. Now I've told Dad, and you're going to hear it, too. If you two don't start behaving like rational adults, you're going to both end up alone. Is that what you really want?"

"Better alone than being handed over to some fur trapper for those long winter nights they have up there," Elizabeth muttered.

"You know," Jessica said suddenly, losing the last remaining vestiges of patience, "you two deserve each other!" She flung open the screen door, escaping to the small brick terrace out back.

"Bad day?" a deep voice inquired blandly.

Jessica stopped in her tracks, staring down at Quinn, who appeared perfectly at home in a white wrought-iron chair. "What are you doing here?"

"I brought Mallory a book on film editing."

"You went out and bought my daughter a book?"

"No, it was one I already owned. I took a few film classes at USC," he revealed. "In LA, it's de rigueur to graduate with at least one cinema class on your transcript."

His green eyes swept over her, from the top of her auburn head down to her stocking-clad feet. "Why don't you sit down?" he suggested amiably, as if it was his backyard and not hers. "You look beat."

"Thanks," Jessica muttered. "It's nice to know I'm so appealing. However, I doubt if I'd ever come up to Pamela Stuart, even on the best of days."

Quinn's jaw hardened and a strange look came into his eyes as he took a long swallow of the Scotch Elizabeth had obviously served him. "Now I understand why you were so abrupt on the phone today. The gossipmongers don't waste any time, do they?"

Jessica was suddenly unbearably exhausted and sank into a chair, stretching her legs out in front of her. She sipped her wine slowly, pretending to have great interest in the ivy climbing the fence.

"Is it true?" she asked finally.

"Would it matter?"

"I don't know. . . . I think so," she admitted softly.

Quinn twirled the ice cubes absently in the glass, his attention directed into the dark amber depths. "If our relationship is strictly business, why would it make any difference who I'm sleeping or not sleeping with?"

"It doesn't," she retorted, rising abruptly. "Forget I even brought it up. Where are the girls?"

"I sent them out for pizza," he answered. "Sit down, Jess. Let's get this out in the open."

"There's nothing to discuss." Despite her argumentative tone, Jessica sat back down in the chair, unaware that her pale face was a study in vulnerability.

Quinn sighed heavily. "What am I going to do with you? You keep protesting that you don't want anything to do with me, but every time you look at me with those blue eyes as wide and deep as the sea, I know you're lying through your teeth. You want me, Jess. Every bit as much as I want you."

"How much does Pamela Stuart want you, Quinn?" she asked acidly.

He arched a blond brow. "Jealous?"

She shook her head vigorously. "Not at all. I just don't consider a man who gets himself engaged to a married woman to be a very good influence on my daughters."

Quinn looked inclined to say something, but refrained, instead throwing back his head and tossing off the rest of the Scotch. "You're driving me crazy," he muttered. Then he leaned forward, his elbows braced on his thighs, his hands holding the glass between his legs.

"Pam and I grew up together," he began. "It's an old pattern with her. Every time she breaks up with a guy, she fancies herself in love with me. It gives her the confidence to carry on.... Not everyone can put their lives back together all by themselves the way you managed to do, Jessica."

Jessica fought down the flush created by his openly tender and admiring gaze. "Why does she pick you?" she asked quietly.

Quinn shrugged. "Like I said, it's an old habit. When she got dumped the night before her junior prom, I agreed to fly back to the city from LA and act as her escort, though I always felt more like her big brother. She showed me off that night, pretending I was her college boyfriend from USC."

"That's sad," Jessica murmured, thinking that for all her wealth and beauty, it didn't sound as if Pamela had an overabundance of self-esteem. Jessica remembered the feeling all too well.

"I thought so at the time," Quinn agreed. "That's why I didn't complain." His somber, level gaze held hers. "And that's why I still play along with the charade every few years, hoping that this will be the time she takes my advice and seeks professional help."

Jessica didn't know what to say to that, so she only nodded, feeling as if she was being drawn into the deep green pools caressing her face.

"Am I forgiven?" he asked.

His warm gaze and slow smile were creating havoc with her senses. Jessica felt as if she was suddenly floating out of her depth, and she struggled to maintain her equilibrium.

"How can I stay angry at a man who'd rescue me from home cooking?" She managed a light, slightly ragged laugh.

"Jill assured me she'd quite literally die if forced to eat another one of your mother's meals," Quinn agreed cheerfully, sitting back in the chair.

Jessica breathed a sigh of relief as the sensual mood was effectively broken. "Jill tends to exaggerate. But your chivalry is noted and appreciated."

"Oh, I'm just getting started," he professed, reaching down with a swift movement and taking her foot in his hand.

"Quinn!"

"You're getting a blister," he observed. "Don't you think you ought to get out of these nylons and put on a Band-Aid? I want you in tip-top condition for Saturday night."

"Saturday night?"

His massaging fingers were doing wonderful things to her aching feet as he grinned at her. "How do you ever expect to rise to the exalted ranks of partner and have your name painted on the door of Bennington, Marston, White and Lowell, if you forget such important things like your boss's wedding anniversary party?"

"Oh, God," Jessica groaned. "I did forget all about it. I suppose I have to go."

"You should at least put in an appearance," he concurred.

"I hate things like that," Jessica muttered, knowing that was one more thing she and Quinn Masterson didn't have in common.

He was obviously in his element at formal society affairs. Affairs. That double entendre brought to mind Pamela Stuart, and although Jessica was willing to accept Quinn's story about the unstable heiress, she didn't believe he dated all those other women for altruistic reasons.

"I suppose you have an invitation, too."

Quinn didn't know what had caused Jessica's eyes to darken with that unwelcome pain, but he had a pretty good idea. In her own way, this strong, self-sufficient woman was as fragile as Pam, he realized. She'd been badly hurt and still carried the scars. He'd never bothered to dispute his exaggerated reputation, never caring what people thought about his personal life. Until now.

"I do," he said, standing up.

As Jessica looked up at him, the setting sun sparked her hair with a warm, fiery glow and Quinn had to restrain himself from reaching down and combing his fingers through the thick waves. He couldn't help wondering how those lush strands would feel spread over his chest after making love and the idea caused an aching yearning deep inside him.

Jessica would've had to been blind to miss the blatant desire suddenly flaming in Quinn's green eyes and she remained transfixed, stunned by an answering need. Her eyes darkened to gleaming sapphire and her blood warmed her skin, imbuing her complexion with the hue of a late summer rose.

"Come here." Quinn's voice was unusually husky as he extended his hand toward her.

As if in a trance, Jessica reached out, allowing her hand to be swallowed up by the one so much larger and stronger. Quinn brought her to her feet, into his arms, fitting her intimately against him as he gave in to impulse and buried his lips in the fragrant softness of her fiery hair. The scent reminded him of springtime—of flower-strewn meadows, fruit trees in full blossom, the rich warmth of sunshine returning after a long gray winter.

"Ah, Jess," he said on a sigh. "I promised myself I wouldn't push, but I think I'm going to go crazy if I can't kiss you."

She lifted her head, a slight, unmistakable smile teasing at her lips. "What's stopping you?" she asked softly.

"Sweetheart," he groaned, "I thought you'd never ask."

Jessica's head reeled as she breathed in a scent reminiscent of the forest after a rain—a rich, earthy aroma laced with the sharper tang of redwoods. Her arms went around his waist as she allowed herself to lean against his rugged strength.

Then he was kissing her, his lips hard and hungry, his tightly leashed control disintegrating into a mindless passion. Jessica had been expecting something gentler, something more cautious. She opened her mouth to object, but at her shuddering soft cry, his tongue slipped past the barrier of her teeth, into the velvet vault beyond, creating havoc with her senses as it swept the moist, dark interior.

Jessica's initial shock disintegrated, replaced by an emotion more vital, more electric than anything she'd ever known. Enticed by the expert sensuality of his kiss, she grew more intrepid, allowing her own tongue to venture forth, at first tentatively, then with increasing boldness, discovering the brisk taste of cinnamon mingling enticingly with a darker, stronger taste of the imported Scotch.

He was a wonderful kisser, she considered through her whirling senses. She could stay here in his arms for the rest of her life. His breath was warm and oh, so seductive as his lips scorched a path from one ravished corner of her mouth to the other. Jessica went up on her toes to run her fingers through his sun-gilt hair.

The movement fitted her feminine frame more closely to his body and as Quinn's hands roamed down her back, they caused little sparks to dance between each vertebra. She could feel the warmth emanating from his body, creating a glow that spread outward from her middle regions, flowing through her blood, warming her fingers, making her breasts ache with unaccustomed heaviness, spiraling downward to her toes.

"You feel good," he murmured, dragging his lips away to blaze a heated trail down the slender column of her neck. "So good..."

Jessica's pulse trebled its rhythm as Quinn's palms cupped her breasts, his thumbs creating an evocative pattern that brought the tight crests surging against the amber silk of her blouse.

Jessica struggled to maintain some slim vestige of sanity, telling herself that if she didn't regain control, not only her mother but her daughters, as well, would soon witness Jessica and Quinn making love on the tiny brick terrace. Even as her body clamored for release, her mind tried to make itself heard, reminding her that she and Quinn were not alone. She had no business behaving like an absolute wanton with this man.

She buried her head in his shoulder, taking deep, calming breaths of air. "Another minute of that and I would have suffocated," she complained on what she hoped was a light note. She failed miserably.

Quinn knew Jessica had been affected as intensely as he by the ardent kiss. Probably even more so. He had talked to Pamela today, seeking information about Jessica, and although his longtime friend had pouted prettily, she had assured him that as far as anyone knew, Jessica had been living the life of a nun since her divorce. She was a remarkably passionate woman; Quinn was surprised she'd been able to keep the floodgates closed for as long as she had.

Quinn felt Jessica gathering up her self-control, wrapping it about herself like a heavy protective cloak. Deciding she had enough problems for now, he opted to match her casual attitude, but was slightly more successful.

"You're supposed to breathe through your nose. But don't worry, a little more practice and you're bound to get the knack of it."

"I don't need any more practice." Her eyes gave him a warning he chose to ignore.

"You're right," he agreed. "You're perfect just the way you are."

His dark gaze made Jessica's legs weaken, and she couldn't muster up the sharp response she knew he deserved. The slam of the front door signaled the return of her daughters, and Jessica heaved a huge sigh of relief as she extricated herself from his arms.

"The girls are back," she stated unnecessarily.

"It appears so." Quinn reached out and looped an auburn strand of hair behind her ear before tilting her chin toward him in a way that effectively captured her gaze.

"I've waited a long time for you," he said suddenly, his husky voice fracturing the silence. "I suppose I can wait until after the pizza."

"You've only known me three days, Quinn," Jessica answered dryly. "So if you think you're going to impress me with your self-restraint, you're sadly mistaken."

"That's where you're way off base," he countered in a serious tone. "I've waited my entire life for you, Jessie O'Neill. And if you think I'm going to let you walk away, now that I've found you, you're dead wrong."

He bent his head, planting a quick, hard kiss on her lips. "Let's eat." Quinn's eyes were laughing as he suddenly noticed her disheveled appearance. "You'd better tuck in your blouse," he warned, "or we'll have some heavy explaining to do to the troops."

Jessica's fingers shook as she tried to shove the amber silk back into her waistband. She finally managed the task, then, pasting a composed expression onto her face, returned to the kitchen, refusing to allow anyone to see that Quinn's statement had shaken her to her toes.

6

EXCUSING HERSELF Jessica ran upstairs to change. When she returned to the kitchen and found Elizabeth sharing the thick, gooey pizza, she was unable to resist a slight gibe.

"I see you're willing to risk a few additives, Mother."

"Quinn is very persuasive," Elizabeth replied serenely. "He assured me that pizza is actually very nutritious."

Jessica wasn't surprised; she'd already witnessed how persuasive the man could be when he put his mind to it. Which was precisely her problem, she considered ruefully. She had no intention of becoming involved with any man; at this point in her life all her energies had to be directed toward her family and building a career.

Shrugging off the problem for the moment, she went over to the refrigerator, taking out a diet cola.

"If you keep feeding me this way," she complained, "I'm going to have to roll down the hill to work in the morning."

He grinned. "I'd say you've got a few pounds to go before we have to ship you off to a fat farm."

"Mom's taken up jogging," Mallory informed him. "She says sitting around an office all day is giving her middle-aged spread."

Jessica could have cheerfully strangled her middle daughter for revealing that little bit of information, but Quinn's gaze, as he submitted her to a slow appraisal, was sparked with masculine approval.

"She hides it admirably," he stated, his eyes lingering on the curves displayed by the snug, well-worn jeans.

"Would you all stop talking about me as if I wasn't here?" she protested, feeling as if she was on public display.

There was a murmured chorus of apologies as she sat down at the table, and Jessica knew she was being overly sensitive. But she didn't retract her complaint.

The conversation turned to the day's events, and Jessica was honestly surprised at how interested Quinn appeared as her daughters related their individual triumphs and small failures. Jill was particularly despondent over the grade on her latest math test, insisting that she never would understand plane geometry.

"Give me one good reason why I will ever need to know the area of an isosceles triangle," she grumbled.

"You've got me," Jessica admitted. "I nearly failed geometry myself. I think the teacher finally felt sorry for me and gave me a passing grade just to get me out of his class."

"I've got a makeup test tomorrow and I know I'm going to fail."

"I can help you memorize theorems again," Mallory suggested, picking up a piece of pepperoni that had slid onto the table.

Despite their differences, her daughters could be very supportive of one another when the chips were down, Jessica observed with an inward smile.

"I know them all by heart," Jill complained. "I just don't know what to *do* with them." Her expression was absolutely bleak.

"Don't look at me," Sara said. "I've just figured out mixed fractions."

The mood around the table was decidedly gloomy when Quinn cleared his throat. "I always liked geometry," he offered almost tentatively.

"You would," Jessica muttered, wishing the man wasn't so damn perfect.

Jill's expression was that of a drowning man suddenly offered a life preserver. "Do you think you could help me study?" she asked hopefully.

Jessica broke in before Quinn had a chance to respond. "I'm sure Mr. Masterson has better things to do with his evening than spend it studying plane geometry," she stated firmly.

"No, actually I don't," he countered calmly. "If you'd like, Jill, I'd enjoy spending the evening here. With all of you."

Jill looked as if she'd just gotten her Christmas present eight months early. Elizabeth's expression reminded Jessica of a very fat cat sitting there with feathers sticking out of its mouth. Mallory and Sara exchanged a long, knowing glance, then eyed their mother, their bright eyes offering congratulations.

They'd obviously all ganged up on her and Jessica knew she'd appear like the Wicked Witch of the West if she offered a single objection. She reluctantly kept her mouth shut, wondering how she was going to keep Quinn Masterson out of her life, when she couldn't even keep him out of her house.

Lost in the problem, she allowed the conversation to continue on around her, no longer pretending an interest. The shrill demand of the phone jolted her out of her troubled musings.

"Jessica," the deep voice said as she picked up the receiver, "how are you?"

"I'm fine, Brian," she replied, drawing interested gazes from the other occupants of the room. "How are you?"

"Fine, fine. Deirdre's fine, too."

As if she cared, Jessica considered with concealed irritation.

"How are the girls?"

"They're fine, too. Do you want to talk to them?"

"I'd love to," her former husband said, "but I'm on my way out the door. I just wanted to see if you'd be willing to change weekends with me."

Jessica shrugged. "I don't see why not."

"Terrific. Thanks a lot, Jess. You're a lifesaver. I'll pick them up tomorrow after school, all right?"

"I'll have everything packed," she agreed absently, uncomfortable with Quinn's thoughtful gaze locked onto her face. She turned her back, fiddling with the telephone cord.

"Great, just great," Brian enthused. "You sound a little tired. Is everything all right? How's work?"

"Everything's fine," she murmured. "Look, Brian, we're eating dinner. The girls will see you tomorrow, okay?"

"Tomorrow," he agreed. "Will you be at the house when I pick them up?"

"I don't know," she hedged. While Jessica had done her best to maintain a friendly relationship with Brian for the girls' sake, she continued to feel uncomfortable in his presence. It brought back too many painful memories. "I may have to work late."

"Oh." He sounded vaguely disappointed. "Well, don't overdo it. You know what they say about all work and no play."

"They say it pays the bills," she countered briskly. "I've got an electrician coming next month who doesn't do charity work."

"I still don't understand why you didn't just keep the house, Jessica. It wasn't that I didn't offer to let you have it."

"I wanted a change," she replied. "We like living in the city."

"I'm not so sure it's good for the girls."

"Was there anything else you wanted?" she asked, firmly closing the door on the argument they'd had far too many times in the past three years.

"Stubborn as always, aren't you?" He didn't bother to hide his irritation.

"That's what I'm told," she agreed. "I'll see the girls are ready."

"Yeah, you do that," he muttered. "Goodbye, Jessica."

"Goodbye." She hung up the phone, forcing down the aggravation she knew was etched onto every taut line in her face.

"You're spending this weekend with your father," she announced, returning to the table.

"This weekend! I can't," Mallory wailed. "You'll have to call him back."

"I won't do any such thing," Jessica said firmly. "Besides, he said he was on the way out the door when he called."

"I'm not going." She folded her arms across her chest.

Jessica knew that of all her daughters, Mallory was the only one who still held a grudge against her father for leaving his family for another woman. She'd done her best never to say anything derogatory about him in her daughters' presence, but the relationship between Brian and his middle daughter was strained, at best. Which was especially unfortunate when she considered that Mallory had always been Brian's favorite. Although Jessica suspected Mallory was suffering her own feelings of personal rejection, she'd never gotten her daughter to discuss it openly.

"Honey," she coaxed, "you always have a good time once you get there."

A mutinous expression hardened the young face. "I had plans for this weekend."

"Plans?"

"The Charlie Chaplin film festival at the Orpheum," she reminded her mother.

She'd talked about little else all month, Jessica recalled belatedly, knowing how excited Mallory had been about the chance to view the comedian's old films.

"I forgot," she admitted. "But as it turns out, I have to work Saturday morning, anyway."

"Gran can take me," Mallory suggested, her gaze as appealing as a cocker spaniel puppy.

"I'm sorry, dear," Elizabeth said. "But I have to go down to Monterey this weekend. I'm decorating a new resort hotel and the owners are flying in from Houston to see what I've planned."

Tears welled up in Mallory's eyes, and the legs of her chair scraped on the oak floor as she pushed it away from the table.

"Terrific," she ground out harshly. "Everyone has their important plans. Why should I expect anyone to care what I want to do?"

Jessica shook her head, knowing that while Mallory was overreacting, her feelings were genuine. "I'm sorry, honey," she apologized. "I promise we'll go next time."

Mallory burst into tears, running from the room. "There won't be any next time," she wailed.

An uncomfortable silence settled over the room and Jessica sighed, pushing back her own chair. "Excuse me," she murmured, following her daughter from the kitchen.

Mallory was lying on her bed, sobs pouring forth from deep in her chest. As Jessica tried to soothe her, it crossed her mind that her daughter's dramatic performance had undoubtedly solved the problem with Quinn. He was probably on his way out the door about now, thankful that he hadn't gotten involved with a middle-aged woman and her three volatile children.

As usual, he surprised her. Jessica heard a slight sound and looked up to see him standing in the doorway.

"May I make a suggestion?"

"It's not necessary," Jessica said quickly, guessing what he had in mind."

Mallory looked up, rubbing at her wet cheeks with the backs of her hands. "What suggestion?" she asked hopefully.

Oh, God, Jessica thought, *don't let her start counting on Quinn. She's already been hurt enough.*

He entered the small bedroom, sitting down on the edge of the bunk bed. "Why don't you and I go to the film festival while your mother's working?"

"Mom?" Mallory's expression begged acquiescence.

"I've already promised your father you'd spend the weekend with him," she protested weakly.

"That's no problem," Quinn assured her. "Let her go to her father's tomorrow night and I'll pick her up and take her into town Saturday morning, then deliver her back to Mill Valley in the afternoon."

Mallory's wobbly smile was beatific. "That's a wonderful idea," she enthused. "Please, Mom."

Jessica shook her head. "I can't allow you to go out of your way for us like that," she said firmly.

"Mom!"

"It's a practical solution, Jess," he argued. "Besides, I can't think of anything I'd rather do than date two gorgeous women in the same day."

"Two?" Mallory asked, sniffling inelegantly.

Quinn handed her a white handkerchief from his pocket. "Two," he agreed. "I'm taking your mother out dancing Saturday night."

Suddenly they were no longer alone. Jill entered the room, followed by Sara. Elizabeth remained in the doorway.

"Mom never goes dancing," Sara offered.

Quinn grinned. "That's where you're wrong, sweetheart," he argued lightly. "Your mother and I danced together once before."

"Really?" Mallory asked, sitting up cross-legged on the mattress, her curiosity getting the better of her self-pity. "After she and Dad got divorced?"

"Before they were even married," Quinn answered. "My big mistake was not grabbing on to a good thing when I saw it. I never should have let your father get first dibs."

"Wow," Jill breathed, her eyes wide. "That's the most romantic thing I've ever heard!"

"At your age, everything is the most romantic thing you've ever heard," Jessica said dryly. "And for your information, I was all of eight years old."

"That was years and years ago," Sara piped up, making Jessica feel absolutely ancient. "And you still remember?"

"Every minute," Quinn asserted, treating Jessica to a particularly warm gaze, which did not go unnoticed by their audience.

"That's because he probably still hasn't recovered," Jessica insisted, rising from the bed to get a little farther away from Quinn. "I spent the entire time crushing his toes."

"You were left-footed," Elizabeth remembered. "Madame Sorenson never could teach you to follow properly."

"See," Jessica said to Quinn, her look saying I told you so. "Why on earth would you want to subject yourself to another evening of being stepped on?"

His slow smile made her blood simmer. "I'll buy a pair of steel-toed shoes," he promised. His gaze returned to Mallory. "So is it a date?"

"Mom?"

Unable to resist Mallory's blatant pleading, Jessica merely shrugged. "Since I seem to be outvoted once again, I suppose it's all right," she agreed reluctantly.

Quinn stood up, rubbing his hands together as if he'd never expected any other outcome. "Terrific. Now, Jill, what do you say we get started on that homework?"

"All right!" she said instantly, picking up the thick textbook from the floor where she'd obviously flung it in a fit of desperation. "We can work in the den, okay?"

"Fine with me," he replied amiably, following her out the door.

A moment later, Jill was back, flinging her arms enthusiastically around Jessica's waist. "I don't know where you found him, Mom. But I'm sure glad you did."

Then she was gone, her face wreathed in a brilliant smile. "It's not what you think," Jessica insisted, uncomfortable with her two remaining daughters' and her mother's knowing smiles. "There's absolutely nothing going on between Quinn and me. So don't anyone go jumping to conclusions!"

"I wouldn't think of it, dear," Elizabeth murmured, a secretive light flickering in her blue eyes.

Jessica couldn't stand any more of the silent scrutiny. "I've got work to do," she stated briskly, marching from the room.

She spent the remainder of the evening locked in her bedroom, attempting to work on the environmental group's brief. She didn't even come out when Elizabeth knocked on the door, informing her that Jill had managed to unravel the secrets of the Pythagorean theorem and Quinn was leaving.

"I'm sure he can find his way out by now," Jessica muttered under her breath, earning an exasperated sigh from her mother as Elizabeth returned downstairs to join in the chorus of good-nights.

TO JESSICA'S RELIEF, the following morning flew by, remaining blissfully uneventful. She experienced a sense of satisfaction as she crossed one item after another off her lengthy list. A few minutes before noon, she was staring down at the pa-

per, debating whether or not to skip over the errand she'd
capriciously scribbled down this morning.

The one thing Jessica had always hated most in the world,
with the understandable exception of a trip to the dentist, was
clothes shopping. That initial dislike had been amplified by
the fiasco with Deirdre Hanson. More than three years later,
Jessica was still relying solely on the clothing her husband's
second wife had selected for the campaign. The last time
Elizabeth had managed to coax Jessica into a department
store was eighteen months ago. She'd suffered a horribly
embarrassing anxiety attack and had no interest in repeating
the experience.

Still, she considered, tapping her pen thoughtfully on the
paper, Quinn's appreciation of her appearance the other night
was etched onto her mind, making her smile whenever she
remembered the sensual gleam in his green eyes. It had been
a long time since a man had looked at her in that way, even
longer since she'd experienced an answering response. As
long as both of them understood that nothing could come of
their relationship but a brief, enjoyable affair, could it be so
wrong to see him from time to time on a social basis?

And, she mused, continuing along that train of thought,
if she was going to have an affair with Quinn, wasn't it only
natural to want to look her best? To feel desirable?

She took a brief mental inventory of her closet, knowing
that the evening dresses encased in clear plastic were expensive, chic and timeless in design. Deirdre had seen to that. But
those clothes belonged to another time. Another Jessica
O'Neill. If she was going to do something as uncharacteristic
as have a fling with a man whose reputation made Casanova's seem tame by comparison, Jessica wanted something
new. Something of her own choosing.

Telling Paula she was taking a long lunch, Jessica left her
office, taking the bus to Macy's Union Square. While many

cities had experienced a deterioration of their downtown area, the four-block hub surrounding Union Square housed an abundance of elegant stores and richly decorated shops. The names of many prestigious New York stores appeared over several doors, especially along Post Street.

But as the bus approached Union Square, Jessica began to experience a creeping sense of anxiety. Her breathing quickened and suddenly the half-filled bus seemed horribly claustrophobic. She reached up, pulling the cord to direct the driver to stop. Once outside on the sidewalk, she took in deep gulps of air, willing her body to relax.

She told herself that she was a strong, independent woman who should certainly be able to go shopping on her lunch hour without falling apart. But as she walked down Post Street, the street became too narrow, the sidewalks too crowded, the buildings tall and menacing as they towered over her. People jostled her as they walked by in the hurried stride demonstrative of San Franciscans. Everyone seemed to have a purpose, a destination, as they strode past, speaking in a wide variety of native tongues.

Jessica wanted desperately to return to the safety of her office, where she was able to remain in control, where she wouldn't feel as if she'd go spinning off the globe at any moment. But something kept her from turning back.

By the time Jessica reached Macy's, her scalp was beginning to burn as if she had hot coals under her hair. Dizziness, chills, shakiness—all the classic symptoms of an anxiety attack returned and she closed her eyes for a moment, leaning against a wall just inside the door. Her distressed state drew the attention of a young salesclerk.

"Are you all right, ma'am?"

The woman's voice seemed to be coming from the bottom of the sea, but Jessica forced herself to concentrate, to carefully watch the full red lips move as she attempted to decipher the words.

Embarrassment threatened to overcome anxiety as she nodded slowly, taking a deep, calming breath. "Yes," she mumbled. "I'm fine," she said a bit more firmly.

"Are you certain?" Lovely slanted dark eyes viewed Jessica with a very real concern.

"Positive," Jessica assured her, standing up a little straighter. "Could you tell me where I can find the Laura Ashley section?"

"Laura Ashley?" The woman's gaze moved over Jessica's severely tailored suit.

"That's right," Jessica said, managing a smile. "I'm in the mood for something romantic."

An hour and a half later, Jessica was watching the salesclerk ring up the results of her uncharacteristic shopping spree. Handing over her charge card, she experienced a sense of pride that could have only come with scaling Mount Everest. Without any help from the ultrachic saleswoman, she'd chosen a glorious selection of clothing that captured the romantic spirit of a bygone era. More important, she'd overcome the ridiculous anxiety that had been the final lingering result of her marriage breaking up. Instructing the store to have the purchases delivered to her home, she was practically floating on air as she returned to the office.

"It must have been one terrific lunch," Paula observed, taking in Jessica's bright eyes and flushed face. "Anyone I know?"

"I was shopping," Jessica said on a laugh.

"You must have found some real bargains."

"There wasn't a bargain in the bunch. In fact, I'm going to be in debt for the next two years. Lucky for me the girls love hot dogs."

Her secretary shrugged. "Well, whatever turns you on, that's what I always say. Your calls are on your desk."

"Anything important?"

"Sylvia Thacker called four times, your mother called once, asking if you'd be home for dinner. Your ex called, reminding you he was picking up the girls at six-thirty, and Mr. Masterson called, but didn't leave a message."

"Would you get Mr. Masterson on the phone?" Jessica asked, her color rising a little higher with her pleasure.

Paula's eyes narrowed, but she refrained from commenting. "Sure."

Jessica slipped off her shoes, tucking her feet under her as she waited for Paula to ring, announcing Quinn was on the line.

"Hi," she said on a slightly breathless tone.

"Hi. You sound in a better mood than you were last night."

"I am," she agreed. "I'm in an absolutely marvelous, wonderful mood."

"Then you probably don't want to hear my news," Quinn warned almost tentatively.

For a fleeting moment, Jessica experienced the very real fear that Quinn was canceling their date. Not that she could blame him; she'd behaved childishly last evening, displaying about as much maturity as she might have expected from Jill.

"Fire away," she said, unaware she was holding her breath.

"Keith Thacker is on the warpath again."

Jessica's relief caused a silvery laugh to bubble forth. "Is that all? What's the problem now?"

"You *are* feeling good today, aren't you?" She could hear the smile in his voice.

"I am," she said. "Not even the Thackers can burst my bubble."

"I've got an idea. Why don't we both take off and go sailing," he suggested suddenly. "Spring is in the air and you know what they say about a man's fantasies."

"I thought that was a man's fancy."

"Fantasies, fancy, what's the difference? I fancy you, Jessie O'Neill. And let me tell you, sweetheart, you definitely improve a man's fantasy life."

Jessica's body warmed to volcanic proportions. "Don't be such a chauvinist," she chided teasingly. "We women have a few fantasies of our own, you know."

Quinn's pleasure was evident. "I suppose it would be asking too much to know that I was featured in any of yours?"

Jessica realized that she was actually flirting with Quinn. Not only that, she was enjoying every minute of it. "Oh, you've got the starring role," she admitted, her tone throaty and inviting.

He groaned. "Do you have any idea what you're doing to me?"

"I can only hope."

"Let's skip the sailing. I've got a better idea."

Jessica smiled, marveling at the way she was able to create that unmistakable desire in Quinn's tone. For the first time in her life, she suddenly felt like Jezebel, Delilah, Salome—all the sensual, alluring femmes fatales who'd known those mysterious tricks that could drive a man insane.

"Save that thought," she purred seductively.

This time Quinn's groan revealed a deep masculine pain. "I suppose that means you're not coming out to play with me today."

"I can't," she confirmed, her own voice displaying her disappointment. "But there's still tomorrow night."

"Tomorrow night," he echoed flatly, as if it was eons away. "I suppose we have to go to that damn party."

"You're the one who pointed out that my appearance is mandatory," Jessica teased. "I remember your instructing me on the politics of getting my name on the door."

"How long do we have to hang around, do you think?"

Jessica chewed thoughtfully on a fingernail, enjoying the idea of Quinn suffering as he waited for her answer. She'd never felt this sense of feminine power with Brian.

In truth, Jessica's self-confidence had been as hard to come by as her independence, but over the past three years, she'd decided she liked the woman she'd become. And apparently, Jessica considered with an inward smile, Quinn did, too.

"I'd say just long enough to put in an appearance," she finally said.

"And the girls are going to be in Mill Valley?"

"With their father," Jessica agreed.

"And your mother's going to Monterey?"

"For the entire weekend."

"So you've got the entire house all to yourself?"

"*We've* got the house all to *ourselves*," she corrected silkily.

"I'm going to die waiting for tomorrow night," he complained.

Jessica laughed lightly. "You can't. I'm counting on you to keep your word and take Mallory to that film festival she has her heart set on."

"Are you sure you can't come?" he asked hopefully. "We could neck in the back row."

"I really do have to work. Sorry."

Quinn heaved an exaggerated sigh. "Well, I guess I'll see you tomorrow night."

He started to hang up when Jessica suddenly remembered he'd called about Keith Thacker's latest complaint. "Quinn, wait a minute," she said quickly.

"Change your mind?"

"Mr. Thacker," she reminded him.

"Oh." His downcast tone indicated it was not his favorite topic of conversation, either. "He's ready to kill Sylvia for shaving that damn dog."

"He was ready to do that yesterday," Jessica said with a shrug.

"He was ready to wring her neck yesterday," Quinn corrected. "Today I think he'd receive a great deal of pleasure in cutting his spiteful wife into little pieces and feeding her to the sharks out in the bay.... It turns out the little guy is suddenly worthless as a stud."

"Why?" Jessica asked curiously. Then she sucked in her breath. "Don't tell me Sylvia had him neutered?"

"Nothing that drastic. But it seems a certain sexy lady Lhasa apso finds bald suitors less than appealing. She refused to have anything to do with him."

Jessica laughed at that, tears welling up in her eyes.

"Hey, it isn't that funny," Quinn complained. "Poor Maximilian is one frustrated male right now." His voice deepened, sounding like ebony velvet. "A state I can empathize with completely."

"He'll just have to suffer until his hair grows back, I suppose," Jessica stated blithely.

"What about me?"

"You have lovely hair, Quinn. Thick and wavy, like spun gold. It's one of those things I like best about you."

"What else do you like?"

The sensuality in Quinn's voice was so palpable that it practically reached through the telephone line to touch her. "I'll tell you tomorrow night," she whispered, suddenly shaken by what she was agreeing to. What she had, in all honesty, invited.

"I'm going to hold you to that, sweetheart," he warned huskily.

"I certainly hope so.... Oh, do you know how to get to the house to pick up Mallory?"

"She gave me directions last night," he answered absently.

"So," he said on a sigh, "are you really working late tonight or hiding from your ex?"

"A little of both," Jessica admitted, not overly surprised by Quinn's accurate perception. There had been more than one occasion when he'd seemed to possess the ability to read her mind.

"I don't suppose you'd like to go out for a late supper?"

"I've got to be at the office early tomorrow morning."

"You realize, of course, you're condemning me to another night spent in a cold, lonely shower."

"I'm sorry."

"She's sorry," he muttered. "I suppose I'd better let you get back to work. Unless you want to talk dirty for a while?"

"Goodbye, Quinn," Jessica said, her smile belying her firm tone.

"Goodbye, Jess." His voice reached out to her like a caress. "I want you to know I'm going to spend the next thirty hours thinking about tomorrow night."

Jessica swallowed. "Me too," she agreed before finally breaking the connection.

Well, she'd done it. Jessica O'Neill, known for her careful, planned life-style, had just agreed to have an affair. As she spent the rest of the day attempting to concentrate on her work, Jessica wondered why, despite the undeniable sense of expectation, that idea made her feel just a little bit sad.

7

JESSICA GREW INCREASINGLY NERVOUS as she prepared for George Bennington's anniversary party. She told herself that at her age, it was ridiculous to be so rattled by the prospect of going out with a man. But it had been a very long time since she'd been out on a date. Fifteen years to be precise.

The term itself was ridiculous. Grown women didn't go out on "dates." There must be another word for what she was about to do. There were several, Jessica thought reluctantly, but she didn't like the sound of any of them. She knew times had changed, knew that there was nothing wrong with exploring the physical desire she'd been experiencing for Quinn Masterson. Yet some nagging little vestige of her upbringing was threatening to take the pleasure from the act.

Nice girls did not go to bed with men they weren't married to, Jessica told herself firmly. All right, she admitted as an afterthought, even in her day, that was not an unknown occurrence. She certainly hadn't been a virgin when she'd married Brian. But she'd loved him—or at least she'd thought she had—and the first time they'd made love had been the result of an unexpected flare of passion. It was certainly not as coldly planned as what she intended to do with Quinn tonight.

As she lay in the tub, surrounded by fragrant bubbles, sipping a calming glass of white wine, Jessica considered that she had spent her entire life seeking other people's approval. She'd been an obedient, studious child, eager for a word of praise or a smile from her larger-than-life father. Terrance MacLaughlin had not spent a great deal of time at home during her childhood; his career had always taken precedence. On those rare occasions that her father was willing to spend time with her, Jessica had never wanted to do anything that might possibly displease him.

She'd continued that same self-destructive behavior in her marriage, dropping out in her second year of law school when Brian insisted that he be the sole breadwinner of his family. He viewed her desire for a career of her own as a threat to his masculine self-esteem. Her place, he had instructed firmly, was home taking care of his house and his children. He'd never be able to love a woman hard-boiled enough to survive the corporate battles found in the real world.

So Jessica, eager to be loved, had acquiesced, creating a comfortable realm where Brian ruled as king, everything revolving around his wishes, his desires. If Jessica experienced resentment from time to time, she assured herself it was a small price to pay to be loved. It was only much later that she discovered what her behavior had cost her in terms of self-esteem and wasted years.

As she sipped the wine slowly, Jessica reminded herself there had been no award ceremonies for wife of the year. No plaques or trophies handed out to "nice girls." When forced out into the high-pressure world that was so different from the peaceful suburban existence she'd known in Mill Valley, she had at first felt like a foreigner in an alien land. She didn't know how to speak the language, play the games.

Jessica had had no idea how one measured accomplishments, judged the constant stream of petty mishaps. For too many years she had measured her success by sparkling windows and pristinely white shirt collars, while a sunken soufflé represented failure. The only things that had remained constant during that time of change were the girls.

Even now, each night before falling asleep, Jessica whispered a short prayer of thanksgiving that they'd avoided the pitfalls so many of her friends' children had fallen prey to. Although her daughters were certainly not the mythical darlings she'd pictured children to be in that romanticized time before motherhood, neither had they ever given her any real cause for concern. In that respect, Jessica figured, she was very lucky.

And she was fortunate to have met a man like Quinn Masterson, she decided, the wine going a little to her head in the warm, humid air of the bathroom. Every woman was entitled to one reckless fling in her life; she'd earned it. Determined to make the most of this weekend, Jessica rose from the tub, her body perfumed with the velvet cling of the bathwater.

She smoothed lotion over every pore, following up with a dusting of talcum powder that left her skin smooth and satiny. She took an unusually long time with her makeup, wanting to appear as feminine as possible, as attractive as she imagined Quinn's usual women to be.

By the time the doorbell rang, Jessica had regained her self-confidence and forced herself to walk slowly downstairs, unwilling to admit her eagerness to see him once again.

Her reward came as Quinn's eyes widened, sweeping over her from the top of her Gibson girl hairstyle, past her slender curves enhanced by the Victorian-style ivory lace gown that swirled about her calves, down to her feet, which were clad in sandals so delicate that they brought to mind Cinderella's glass slippers.

"This," he said, his voice uneven as he moved into the foyer, "was definitely worth the wait."

She smiled, twirling around in the soft glow of the antique wall light. "I'm glad you approve," she murmured, her cheeks flushed with feminine satisfaction that he found her desirable.

"I approved of you in that cute pink running suit," he countered, drawing her into his arms. "I thought you were delightful in that feminine little outfit the other night, and found you sexy as hell in those tight jeans. But this . . ."

He tilted his head back, gazing down at her, his eyes burning . "This is every fantasy I've ever had, come to life."

Jessica's lips curved in a teasing, provocative smile. There was a heady element of power in this situation as she realized how much Quinn wanted her. How much he needed her.

She pressed her palm against his chest, thrilled by the strong beat of his heart beneath her fingertips. "You're not so bad yourself," she murmured, her fingers stroking the front of his pleated white dress shirt.

She could feel his low chuckle. "I'm glad to know I pass inspection."

"Oh, you do," she agreed. "I've always thought men in tuxedos were very sexy."

"Men?" He arched a brow, revealing an unexpected jealous streak that Jessica found absolutely thrilling.

"Don't worry, Quinn," she said, her hands going up to curl about his neck. "Not only do you pass, you set the standard."

They were touching from their chests to their thighs, generating a heat that belied the cool evening temperature.

"You know that you're making it extremely difficult for me to think about your career advancement," he murmured, punctuating his words with light kisses against her lips.

"I know."

"Do you also know that if you keep moving against me that way we'll never get out of here?"

Her fingers were playing in the gilt strands of hair at the back of his neck, her hips moving in seductive little circles against his.

"I know that, too."

"Ah, Jess," he sighed, his breath a warm breeze against her mouth. "You sure picked one hell of a time to pull out the stops."

He kissed her then, a long, lingering kiss that seemed to go on forever. Through her dazed senses, Jessica felt his body trembling with unsatiated desire. His hands moved over her, molding her shape under the lacy dress as if she were malleable clay, and as she dissolved under his touch, Jessica realized that the soft, desperate moans were coming from her own ravaged lips.

All too soon those wonderful, seductive hands moved to her shoulders, putting her a little away from him. "We'd better go," he suggested flatly.

She nodded, her trembling fingers stroking his freshly shaven cheek. "I suppose so," she agreed without a great deal of enthusiasm.

"We won't stay long."

"Just put in an appearance."

"Offer our congratulations."

Her liquid gaze held vast feminine promises. "And then we'll come home."

"Home," he echoed, giving her a short, hard kiss on her pink lips.

"Do me one favor," he said, his voice still far from steady as they drove toward the Benningtons' penthouse apartment.

"Anything," Jessica agreed promptly.

He looked over at her, shaking his head as he gave her a lopsided smile. "Don't look at me that way while we're at the party. Or my resultant behavior may end up getting you canned."

Jessica grinned. "I'll try," she murmured. "But you know, it just might be worth it."

Quinn reached out, taking her hand and lifting it to his lips. "I knew you were a wanton at heart," he professed happily, lowering her hand to his thigh.

Jessica felt light-headed, filled with a strange happiness she'd never known before. "Is that so bad?" she asked, batting her lashes flirtatiously, her fingers stroking the firm muscle under the black dress slacks.

"Honey, I wouldn't have you any other way.... However, if you don't behave yourself, you're going to be forced to walk into that party with a blatantly indecent escort."

"Oh?"

He moved her hand to demonstrate the effect she was having on him. "Any more questions?"

With a forwardness that at any other time would have shocked her, Jessica was in no hurry to retrieve her hand.

"Just one," she said, as he brought the Maserati to a screeching halt in the subterranean parking garage of the building.

"What's that?" he asked raggedly, closing his eyes to her intimate caress.

"Is it time to leave yet?"

Quinn chuckled and picked up her hand, placing it on her own lap. "Behave yourself, wanton," he instructed firmly. Then he leaned his head back, closing his eyes. "Give me a little time," he muttered. "This isn't that easy a task."

Jessica studied the handsome face only inches from hers, watching his smooth brow furrow with concentration, his dark lashes resting against his cheeks, his full lips still curved in a little half smile. A warmth infused her body that went far beyond physical desire, and for a fleeting moment, she thought it might actually be love she was experiencing.

Then she forced that errant, romantic notion to the back of her mind. It was only natural that she was looking for an excuse to justify her uncharacteristic behavior. She had admittedly come a long way in the past three years, but her early socialization went deep. There was obviously still a part of her that needed to feel she was in love before going to bed with a man. That's all it was, the pragmatic side of her nature decided. So long as she recognized this odd feeling for what it was, everything would be all right.

The Benningtons' apartment took up the entire floor of the glittering glass monolith towering above the city, offering a spectacular view of sparkling lights and the darkened waters of San Francisco Bay. The party was in full swing when Jessica and Quinn arrived, and as she viewed the number of people crowding the room, Jessica knew no one would notice if she and Quinn escaped the anniversary celebration early.

"Ms O'Neill!" George Bennington greeted her enthusiastically, as if the unpleasant scene in his office earlier in the week had never occurred. "How nice you were able to attend our little party."

Jessica smiled and shook the outstretched hand of the senior partner and founder of Bennington, Marston, White and Lowell.

"Thank you for inviting me," she answered politely. "I hope my gift arrived."

"I'm sure it did," he replied absently. "Gloria takes care of that type of thing." His gaze moved to Jessica's escort, his eyes narrowing slightly. "Quinn, it's good to see you again."

"Always a pleasure to be invited," Quinn responded. "Congratulations."

"Yes, well, the party was Gloria's idea. To be perfectly honest, I've lost track of the years. It still amazes me we've managed to stay together so long."

"It's an admirable accomplishment in this day and age," Quinn agreed.

"Speaking of which," George stated, "aren't you handling Keith Thacker's divorce?"

"Unfortunately, yes."

"And you, Ms O'Neill, are representing Mrs. Thacker, if I'm not mistaken."

Jessica was not fooled by his casual tone. "That's right."

"Not that I'm questioning your integrity," he qualified his next statement, "but don't you think your, uh, relationship with Quinn might be considered a conflict of interest?"

"Relationship?" Jessica inquired blandly, not willing to help the man out.

Once again she got the distinct impression her employer was not an admirer of women attorneys. How dare he imply that she'd compromise her client because of any feelings she might have for Quinn!

"Ms O'Neill has been representing Sylvia with annoying persistence," Quinn interjected smoothly. "In fact, she's probably the finest champion the woman has found. You don't have a thing to worry about, George." His tone hardened just enough to close the door on that particular subject without being impolite.

George Bennington's smile was irritatingly unctuous and once again Jessica was reminded of Quinn's prowess as an attorney. Obviously, while not caring about her feelings, the older man was reluctant to offend Quinn.

"I'm pleased to hear that," he stated, looking past them to another couple who'd just arrived. "Why don't you two get something to drink?"

"That's a terrific idea," Quinn said, putting his hand lightly on Jessica's back and leading her in the direction of the bar, which had been set up at one end of the vast room.

"The nerve of that man," Jessica spluttered as they walked away. "To even suggest that I'd allow my personal life to interfere with my work!"

"Don't let him get to you," Quinn suggested calmly. "He's always that way with first-year attorneys."

"Women first-year attorneys," she muttered under her breath.

"*All* first-year attorneys," he corrected.

She looked up at him. "How would you know?"

"I spent my first year out of law school at Bennington, Marston and White. Lowell wasn't a partner yet."

"Oh." She was silent for a moment, considering that. "And he was that rough even way back then?"

Quinn chuckled. "You don't have to make it sound like the olden days, you know. Back before dinosaurs roamed the earth. I'm only forty, Jess."

Her irritation melted away and she grinned up at him. "That old?" she asked sweetly. "My goodness you've held your age remarkably well, Quinn." He scowled, causing Jessica to laugh lightly in return. Then her expression turned serious again. "Really, was he so frustratingly unbending when you were there?"

"We called it hell year," he revealed. "And if anything, I think he was even rougher on me." His handsome face turned thoughtful for a moment. "No, I take that back. I know he was rougher on me."

"Why?"

Quinn shrugged. "I suppose it had something to do with bending over backward to demonstrate that family didn't receive preferential treatment."

"Family?" Jessica stared at him blankly.

Quinn arched an incredulous brow. "You didn't know?"

"Know what?"

"That George Bennington is my uncle? I didn't think there was anyone in the legal community who wasn't aware of that little fact."

His words only served to remind Jessica that while Quinn was building his career, she'd been home folding diapers. Now, although she was trying her best to catch up, she secretly wondered if Quinn wouldn't have more in common with someone like Vanessa. Or Pamela Stuart.

Quinn misread her dour expression. "Believe me, honey, it'll get better."

"I certainly hope so," she muttered. "Because to tell you the truth, I've gotten an offer from the D.A.'s office that I'm seriously considering."

"Really?" He looked down at her with renewed interest. "I wouldn't have thought that any woman who starts her day with a detailed list would enjoy the chaos oftentimes found in the D.A.'s office."

"You have to be just as thorough in your work if you want to prosecute," Jessica objected. "Otherwise there'd be no convictions."

"That's true," he agreed amiably. "However, you also have to admit that the ability to punt, when necessary, is a decided asset."

"I'm working on that," Jessica said with a slight smile. "The way I look at it, the Thackers, if nothing else, are a good proving ground."

Quinn chuckled, his eyes warm as he gazed down at her. "You are just one surprise after another, pretty lady."

Jessica's eyes met his, and there was an instant of heat. "Thank you, sir," she said lightly. Then she smiled. "I thought you'd promised me a drink."

"I'd rather ravish your delectable body."

"Your uncle would love that," Jessica said with a musical, happy laugh. As they continued to weave their way through the throng of party guests to the bar, something occurred to her. "If it gets so much better," she challenged, "why did you leave?"

Quinn laughed heartily. "Be truthful, Jess. Can you see George and me working together?"

No, she considered thoughtfully, not at all. They were both incredibly strong-willed men. "I suppose not," she decided aloud.

"You're not the only one who's experienced a need to establish a sense of independence," he stated quietly.

Jessica could read the understanding in his gaze and was trying to think of something to say that would break this silken web that was settling down around them. Then she heard a familiar voice calling her name.

"Dad," she replied with surprise, turning around to view the tall, silver-haired man forging his way through the crowd. "What are you doing here?"

"One of the disadvantages of being an august magistrate in this town is that I get invited to all these bashes," he replied with a grimace. "Hello, Quinn. It's nice to see my daughter's finally latched onto someone who's almost good enough for her."

"Spoken like a properly adoring father," Quinn answered with a broad smile. "How's retirement treating you, Mac?"

"It's the pits," Terrance MacLaughlin confided. "Don't ever retire, Quinn. If I'd known how it was going to change my life, they'd have had to drag me screaming and kicking from the bench."

"It must be quite an adjustment," he agreed sympathetically.

"That's the understatement of the year." Jessica's father took a long swallow of bourbon. "Where's your mother?" he asked suddenly.

"In Monterey."

Terrance "Mac" MacLaughlin muttered a low oath. "I figured she'd be here. That's the only reason I showed up." He ran his finger inside his starched collar. "I've always hated these monkey suits."

"Why did you think Mother would be here?" Jessica inquired curiously.

"She and Gloria Bennington are old friends."

"Perhaps she didn't feel like celebrating a wedding anniversary when you two are having problems," Jessica offered, hoping that her father would admit he'd come here to convince his wife to return home.

"She always was as stubborn as a Missouri mule," Mac grumbled. "And she's gotten a lot worse lately."

"That's the same thing she says about you."

"Sure, take your mother's side, Jessica. You women always stick together, don't you?"

Jessica sighed, putting her hand on her father's arm. "I'm not taking anyone's side," she stated firmly. "I just wish you two would get together and discuss whatever's bothering you."

"I've tried. She won't listen to reason.... Do you know she told me that I drove her crazy? The woman waited forty-six years to let me know I was in her way. Told me to get out of the house and leave her alone." His oath was short and impatient. "Well, I figure Alaska's far enough away that I won't be a nuisance any longer."

"I can't believe Mother said exactly that," Jessica argued. "What were you doing?"

Her father arched a silvery brow. "Are you judging me guilty without a fair hearing, Jessie? Your own father?"

Jessica exchanged a frustrated glance with Quinn who'd wisely remained silent during the interchange. At her silent request, he spoke up.

"Why don't we get you a refill, Mac," he suggested smoothly. "It'll give us a chance to talk man to man." He looked down at Jessica, his green eyes smiling. "You won't mind fending for yourself for a few minutes, will you, sweetheart?"

"Not at all," she answered gratefully. Going up on her toes, she kissed her father's cheek. "It was nice seeing you, Dad. We should get together more often."

"If you're ever in Alaska, look me up," he muttered, allowing himself to be led away by Quinn, who gave Jessica a wink over his shoulder.

"Sweetheart, is it?"

Jessica's shoulders stiffened at the unveiled sarcasm in the deep voice behind her. She slowly turned, eyeing Brian O'Neill. This party was definitely turning into a family reunion, she thought grimly. And this was one former family member she could go all evening without meeting.

"I didn't know you were going to be here."

"Gracious as always, I see."

Jessica refused to respond to her former husband's baiting. "I thought you wanted to be with the girls this weekend. Who's taking care of them? Deirdre?" Despite her best intentions not to show her irritation, Jessica's tone indicated the improbability of that particular scenario.

"Deirdre's in New York on another one of those blasted buying trips of hers. The girls wanted a slumber party with the Franklin kids and I didn't think they needed me around for that. Mrs. Wilson's staying at the house."

"They've missed Bonnie and Lori," Jessica agreed. "So, what are you doing here?"

"You know Bennington handles O'Neill Development's legal work," Brian reminded her. "I received an invitation at the office last week. I wasn't planning to attend until I spent last night and today hearing all about Mr. Wonderful. I decided I'd better warn you about the big mistake you're making."

"I'm not making any mistake," Jessica argued coolly. "But even if I were, Brian, you're in no position to offer advice about my life. You were the one who said I needed to become more independent." She held out her arms. "Meet Jessica O'Neill, modern career woman."

"Modern enough to sleep with a man with my daughters in the next room?" he sneered.

Jessica felt her color rise. "Not that it's any of your business, but I haven't been doing anything that could harm the girls in any way."

"You let Masterson turn their heads with his slick charm. What are they going to do when he dumps you and moves on to his next conquest?"

Jessica pressed her lips together, her blue eyes circling the room, looking for Quinn. She was definitely in need of a drink. Unfortunately he seemed to have disappeared, along with her father. She schooled her tone to appear calm, uncaring.

"I imagine they'll do the same as they did when you dumped me. Carry on."

His dark eyes narrowed. "You never used to be this strong," Brian mused aloud. "A few years ago you would have been running from the room in tears."

"A few years ago, you would have been able to hurt me," she countered.

"And now?"

She shrugged, surprised to find that although Brian admittedly irritated her, she didn't feel any lingering pain. Or any emotion of any kind, for that matter.

"I've grown up."

His gaze darkened as it moved over her, taking in her thick auburn hair, the stylish yet romantic dress, her long legs clad in sheer stockings. Jessica remained still, submitting to his lengthy study, confident that she looked uniquely attractive.

"I can see you have," he murmured. "Since it seems Masterson has deserted you, why don't you let me get you a drink and we'll talk about old times."

The invitation in his deep voice was unmistakable, and rather than being pleased by the fact that her former husband suddenly found her desirable, Jessica was stunned to discover that she felt absolutely nothing.

"This is supposed to be a party, Brian. Not a wake." Glancing around the room, she spotted Quinn headed their way. "Have a good evening," she suggested with a smile, leaving him staring after her as she went to meet Quinn.

"I see you weren't lonely." He didn't bother to hide his annoyance.

She looked up at him curiously. "Are you by any chance jealous?"

"You're damn right I am. I leave you alone for a few minutes and return to find your ex practically eating you up with those beady little eyes. How am I supposed to feel?"

She took his arm and maneuvered through the crowd of guests to the French doors leading out to the balcony. "I think I could use some fresh air."

"The fog's in; it's going to be cool out there," he warned.

Her smile was unmistakably inviting. "Then you'll just have to keep me warm."

The fog had indeed rolled in like a thick blanket, a few stars valiantly managing to make themselves seen as they sparkled in the night sky. A waning moon cast a shadowy, silver light against the top of the Golden Gate Bridge as it thrust its way above the veiled entrance to San Francisco Bay. The sounds of the party drifted away and despite the steady hum of traffic several stories below, Jessica and Quinn could have been the only two people in the world.

"I'm glad Brian was here tonight," Jessica said softly.

"You don't know what that does to my ego," Quinn muttered.

She turned, her back against the railing as she placed her palms on either side of his stern face. "You don't understand," she protested, holding his frustrated gaze with eyes as soft and blue as a tropical lagoon.

"All these years, while I've been building a life for myself, in some little corner of my mind, I've been wanting to become the kind of woman that could compete with the Deirdre Hansons of the world. The type of modern woman who could interest a man, meet him on an equal basis."

"So now you've discovered you've made it. Congratulations. You can steal your husband back from his new wife and it'll be just one happy family again."

Jessica refused to be intimidated by Quinn's icy tone. "Brian did seem honestly interested in me," she admitted. "But the surprising thing was that I didn't care." She shook her head regretfully, her voice quavering ever so slightly. "All these years I'd dreamed of that moment, imagined how I'd feel when I finally earned his approval. Not that I ever thought about going back to him," she stated firmly. "I just wanted him to realize what he'd thrown away without a backward glance."

Quinn was silent for a long time, staring past Jessica out into the billowy mist wrapping itself around the city. "I think I can understand that," he said finally. "So how did it feel?"

Jessica's laugh was rich and full-bodied. "That's the amazing thing. Nothing happened. I kept waiting to feel something—pleasure, vindication, satisfaction. But all I could think about was getting away to find you."

"Oh, Jess." One hand cupped her cheek, while the long fingers of the other splayed against her throat, causing her blood to beat against the delicate ivory cameo. "I was ready to kill that bastard when I saw the way he was looking at you. After what he did, he doesn't deserve a second chance.

"You're mine now, Jess," he professed fiercely. "I've waited too long for you to give you up now."

The possessive statement tolled a warning in the back of Jessica's mind, but she was given no time to consider Quinn's huskily stated words as his mouth fused with hers, scorching away all reason.

The night breeze was creating havoc to Jessica's carefully coiffed hair, fingers of damp fog brushed against her cheeks, but all she was aware of was the heat of Quinn's mouth, the hardness of his body pressing against hers, arousing the most primitive of womanly instincts as she molded her softness to his rigid strength. She was soaring, flying free and high, meeting Quinn's own desperate desire and surpassing it as a shock of need rocketed through her.

She was beyond thought, beyond reason, crying out softly as Quinn dragged his lips away, breathing heavily as he rested his chin atop her disheveled hair.

"I think we're having an earthquake," he managed to gasp between gulps of air.

Jessica's own breathing was unsteady as she turned her head to press a kiss against his neck. "I don't care," she whispered, her lips plucking at the warm, slightly scratchy skin. "I want to make love with you, Quinn."

"Here? That'd be a bit dangerous, darlin', even discounting the earthquake."

"I feel like being reckless tonight. Let's live dangerously, Quinn." Her fingers were toying with the onyx studs on his shirt.

"You are living recklessly, Jess," he murmured, lifting her hand to his lips and eyeing her seriously over the top of their linked fingers. "I don't think you begin to realize what you're starting here."

Her soft smile was provocative and definitely enticing. "Why don't we go home and put your theory to the test, counselor?"

Quinn suddenly realized how Adam must have felt when Eve waved that bright red apple under his nose. She still didn't understand. He wanted her—he wasn't about to deny that. But he wanted more than Jessica's body, as lovely and desirable as it was. He wanted her heart. And yes, dammit, he considered almost fiercely, he wanted her soul.

He understood that she'd suffered with the breakup of her marriage. He realized that she'd undergone a significant metamorphosis in order to become the self-sufficient attorney she was today. He ached for her loss, just as he was pained by her apparent inability to realize that love didn't equal weakness, marriage didn't have to mean subjugation.

Quinn wanted to spend the rest of his life with Jessica. He wanted it for himself, but he wanted it for her, as well. And her daughters. He knew they could be a family, if she'd only let things take their natural course. If she'd only open her eyes to the love he had to offer.

If he gave in to temptation and took Jessica to bed tonight, he'd only be muddying the waters, allowing her to confuse sex with love. If he wanted to play this thing the smart way, he'd wait until she was ready to admit the feeling she had for him couldn't be anything else but love. But God, how he wanted her!

What the hell, Quinn considered with an accepting, inward shrug as he took Jessica's hand and let her lead him back into the room to the front door. He never claimed to be bucking for sainthood.

8

As Quinn guided the Maserati through the fogbound streets, Jessica experienced a sense of anticipation like nothing she'd ever known. She was actually going to do it, she realized. She was going to have a cold-blooded, casual affair.

Not that there was anything cold-blooded about Quinn, she mused, surreptitiously studying him as he drove. He radiated a masculinity so strong, so powerful, so heated that there had been times it had threatened to overwhelm her. She trembled just thinking about the way his touch could bring her blood to flame.

"Cold?"

Those sharp green eyes didn't miss a thing, she thought. Jessica shook her head, meeting his questioning gaze. "No," she admitted on a whisper. "I think I'm burning up."

He treated her to a slow, sensual smile. "Don't feel like the Lone Ranger."

Her hand had been resting on his knee and now he covered it with his, entwining their fingers, his thumb stroking little circles against the sensitive skin of her palm. Jessica felt herself melting into the glove-soft leather seat.

"Your dad's having a hard time adjusting to retirement," he revealed, as if he found it necessary to turn the conversation to something more casual in order to survive the short drive to Jessica's town house.

"Is that what you two were talking about?"

"That. And other things. He thinks quite highly of you, by the way. I had to promise my intentions were honorable."

Jessica felt the embarrassed flush staining her cheeks and was grateful for the cover of darkness. "I hate to have you lie to him," she murmured. "But it's probably for the best."

He slanted her an appraising glance. "What makes you think I was lying?"

Jessica was horrified by the way those simple words managed to pierce her self-protective armor. No, she warned herself, she couldn't allow her desire for the man to cloud her resolve. This was a fleeting, transitory relationship. A night, a weekend, a month at the very most. Surely in thirty long days this attraction would run its course. Little habits would begin to grate on nerves, passions would cool, irritations would set in. Jessica was a realist; she knew that happily ever after was a myth originated in fairy tales, perpetuated by romantic storytellers.

"Did he say anything about the reason for Mother leaving their house?" she asked, changing the subject.

Quinn stifled the urge to shake her until those lovely teeth rattled. He'd always thought of himself as being single-minded, but Jessica's stubbornness surpassed anything he'd ever known.

"It seems that in an effort to make himself useful, he rearranged her office."

"Oh, no," Jessica groaned, recalling the cluttered chaos that Elizabeth had always worked in. Although others might wonder how she ever found anything in the muddle of wallpaper samples, paint chips and bolts of fabric, her mother had always possessed the ability to locate a desired swatch of material without a moment's hesitation.

"While she was in Houston last week, meeting with those developers, he installed shelves on all four walls and, as he so succinctly put it, 'tidied things up a bit for her.'"

"I imagine she was thrilled," Jessica said dryly.

"According to Mac, she stared at his remodeling for about ten minutes, then, telling him exactly what he could do with his handiwork, left the house without even bothering to unpack."

"I can't believe she'd throw away forty-six years of marriage just because of a few shelves. No matter how angry she was."

Quinn shrugged. "I think it was just the last straw. Apparently they've been arguing about what she calls his interference for the past six months since his retirement. Mac, of course, only sees himself as trying to help. I think he's at loose ends these days."

"Poor Dad," she murmured. "I know how it is to feel useless."

Quinn didn't comment on that, instead squeezing her fingers reassuringly. "Give them time to work it out," he advised. "If I tell you something in confidence, promise you won't warn Elizabeth?"

"I promise."

"He's on his way to Monterey."

Well, Jessica considered, that was something. "I hope he uses a little more finesse when he tries to convince her to return home," she stated thoughtfully. "I don't think Mother will respond to his usual steamroller tactics."

"Like mother, like daughter," Quinn murmured, pulling up to the curb in front of her house. He sat still for a long, silent moment, leaning his forearms on the steering wheel, staring out into the well of darkness beyond the windshield. When he finally turned to look at Jessica, his gaze was unnervingly somber.

"I don't want to push you into anything tonight, Jess," he said quietly, his green eyes locked onto her face. "If we make love, I need to know that you want me as much as I want you."

She leaned forward, brushing his lips with her own. "Let me show you exactly how much I want you, Quinn," she whispered, her warm breath fanning his face as she rained kisses over his stern features.

Muffling a groan, Quinn needed no further invitation.

Jessica was suddenly unreasonably nervous as they entered the house. "Would you like a drink?" she offered.

"Sounds nice," Quinn agreed amiably.

"I think there's some white wine in the refrigerator," she said. "But if you'd rather have Scotch, or brandy, or something else . . ." Her voice drifted off.

"Whatever you're having is fine."

She turned in the direction of the kitchen, then stopped. "I don't want anything to drink," she said softly.

"I don't, either," he admitted, taking her hand as they climbed the stairs.

The house was too quiet, and Jessica found herself longing for some of Jill's pulsating rock music to break the thick silence.

"I never thanked you for taking Mallory to that film festival today," she said.

"I had a good time," Quinn replied easily. "Mallory did, too, I think. Although your mother would have definitely disapproved of our behavior."

"Oh? Why?"

He grinned down at her. "Do you have any idea how much popcorn and candy an eleven-year-old can consume? Just imagine the additives."

Jessica laughed, as she was supposed to. She was grateful to Quinn for lightening the mood.

His eyes widened as he entered Jessica's bedroom, although he wondered why he was surprised by the brilliant canvases hanging on her walls.

"You painted those, didn't you?" he asked, already knowing the answer as he studied the bright, abstract swirls of color.

"When I was married," she agreed, unreasonably anxious for his opinion. "Mother cringes every time she walks into the room. She says they clash horribly with the Victorian floral wallpaper."

"It suits you," he replied, his gaze circling the decidedly feminine room, then returning to Jessica's softly flushed face. "You've got a lot of unbridled passion lurking under that enticingly delicate exterior, Jessie."

So thrilled was she by the desire burning in Quinn's dark gaze that Jessica forgot her usual assertion that she was a strong, independent woman. At this moment, she only wanted him to find her desirable.

"I'm glad it's you," she said quietly, moving into his arms.

Quinn looked down at her questioningly.

"It's been a very long time," she explained, faltering a bit as she succumbed to the lambent desire she viewed in those green eyes. "I didn't want to do this with just anybody. It seemed important that it was someone I . . ."

Her voice drifted off as she tried to come up with the proper word. *Not love*, she told herself firmly. Love implied commitment, demands, weakness. She couldn't allow herself to yield to its false, ethereal promises.

Quinn waited patiently, feeling Jessica's inner struggle as she tried to sort out her feelings. One part of him wanted to kill Brian O'Neill for leaving Jessica so wounded, so afraid to trust. Another part of him was thankful that the guy hadn't realized a terrific thing when he had it. If Jessica's idiot of a husband hadn't left her, she and Quinn might never had met. What a void that would have left in his life!

"Care for," she finished weakly, resting her forehead against the firm line of his shoulder.

Well, it wasn't precisely what he'd wanted to hear. But it was enough. For now.

His hands moved to her hair, pulling out the mother-of-pearl combs that held it in precarious order, his fingers sifting through the fiery waves as they tumbled down over her shoulders.

"I love your hair down," he murmured, grazing the fragrant softness with his lips. "You remind me of something from an eighteenth-century novel."

Her full lips curved in a slight smile as she tilted her head back to look up at him. "Ah," she said on a slight sigh, "we're going to play lusty aristocrat and naughty milkmaid."

His fingers toyed with the cameo at her throat, finding the catch and releasing it. "Uh-uh," he argued, opening the lacy frill at her neck to press his lips against her skin. Jessica's pulse leaped in response. "You're every inch an aristocrat, sweetheart. The kind of woman who instilled all that passion in pirates and gamekeepers."

Jessica felt her legs weakening as he slowly began to unbutton her dress, his lips grazing each new bit of freed skin, tasting her warming flesh, drinking in a sweet scent that reminded him of lilacs in April. He took his time manipulating the pearl buttons through the silk loops, like a man unwrapping the most special of gifts.

"This was a bad idea," she whispered, her fingers digging into his shoulders as she clung to him for support.

For a brief, horrible moment, Quinn thought Jessica was about to change her mind. But as her body swayed against him, he decided he might be wrong.

"What was a bad idea?" His tongue was cutting moist swaths down the slope of her breasts, causing an ache that reached to her very core.

"This dress," she complained, flinging her head back, granting him further access to her creamy skin. "I should have found one with a zipper."

He chuckled as the dress finally fell open to her waist. "Anticipation is half the fun," he murmured, taking one pebbled bud between his lips.

Jessica's head was spinning and she was certain she'd faint at any moment. A dizzying excitement raced through her and she thrust her hands into his thick, crisp hair, pressing him against her suddenly moist skin.

The heat seeping into her body was consuming her, licking through her veins, spiraling outward until she thought she'd explode. But still Quinn took his time, moving his head to the other breast, treating it to a torture just as sweet, just as prolonged.

"Quinn, please," she begged, her fingers fumbling with the studs of his dress shirt, anxious for a feel of the hard chest hidden by the crisp white material. She'd never wanted a man like this—never needed a man as much as she needed Quinn at this moment.

He pushed the dress off her shoulders, going down on his knees as he continued to bring it over the soft swell of her hips, down her trembling thighs, to where it finally lay in a lacy puddle at her feet. As if in a trance, Jessica stepped out of the expensive dress, closing her eyes to the sensual torment as Quinn repeated the motion with her silk half-slip. His eyes seemed to burst into flame at what he found waiting for him.

Jessica had allowed her sensuality to run rampant while shopping for this evening, and if she'd been worried that Quinn might find her purchases too contrived, too costumey, that fear dissolved as he viewed the lacy white garter belt, bikini panties and ivory silk stockings that clung to her legs.

"That outfit definitely invites ravishing," he said huskily.

"Oh, yes," she breathed, shaking like a leaf under gale-force winds.

Quinn slipped the sandals from her feet, then began kissing every inch of her long, slender leg, stopping just short of the lacy confection that framed her femininity. He forged a similar trail back down her other thigh, nibbling at the back of her knee, his tongue dampening the silk covering her ankle. A blood-red passion whipped through her and just when she knew she could no longer stand, he slowly lowered her to the bed.

"You're exquisite." His lips trailed over her soft stomach, his voice echoing against her heated flesh. "Everything I've ever imagined." He untied the ribbons at her hips, easily ridding her of the lacy bikini, his fingers forging tantalizing paths on the satin skin at the inside of her thighs.

As Jessica writhed on the bed, her hips arching into his increasingly intimate touch, she realized that she'd completely thrown away her carefully acquired restraint. But as Quinn's lips caressed her sensitive flesh, she knew that whatever she was giving away, she was receiving tenfold.

"Please," she whispered, her voice ragged. "Please make love to me."

Lifting his head, Quinn knew he had never seen anything as beautiful as Jessica's liquid blue eyes, filled with a desire that equaled his own. He held her gaze, his fingers causing havoc to her body as his hand moved up her leg, tracing beguiling patterns on her silk-covered thigh.

"I am," he said simply, lowering his head once again, his lips exploring the skin of her midriff, leaving a raging heat behind. "I knew it."

"Knew what?" she asked weakly, melting under his expert caresses. Jessica was not inexperienced—she'd been married, after all. But she had never known anything like the sweet, aching passion Quinn's hands and lips were releasing from deep within her.

"That your skin would be even silkier than that lacy confection you were wearing." His fingers drew one stocking down the long length of her leg, his lips returning up the trail his hands had blazed. "And you taste so very, very good."

"Quinn," she complained, lifting her hips invitingly off the mattress, "I don't want to wait any longer. I want to make love to you now."

Through the fog clouding her senses, Jessica was stunned to hear herself issuing such a demand. But Quinn had turned her body to flame, and she knew only he could quench the fires threatening to consume her.

"It's not that simple, sweetheart," he murmured as he slowly stripped off the other stocking. "There are certain stages one must go through before reaching the final destination."

Under normal circumstances, Jessica would have agreed. She preferred her life to run in an orderly fashion, but this was ridiculous. She sucked in her breath as he reached under her, his deft fingers manipulating the catch on the lacy garter belt.

"Can't you skip a few steps?" she suggested, quivering under his touch as the passion he'd evoked escalated to exquisite heights.

Quinn could feel Jessica's surrender as she trembled beneath him. Her body was his for the taking, but he had discovered over the past few days that he was a selfish man. He was determined to have all of Jessica O'Neill.

"That would be cheating," he stated with a breezy attitude he was far from feeling, as his lips explored every inch of satiny skin.

Quinn could feel the heat rising from her body in waves as his lips continued their erotic journey. He found himself being irrevocably drawn into his own sensual snare. His blood was pounding in his ears as he explored her welcoming warmth, and as she cried out, he vowed that she'd never forget this night.

Suddenly she was twisting in his arms, practically tearing his clothes from his body as she displayed a hunger and a power just as vital, just as desperate as his own. Her lips and hands moved over Quinn as his had moved over her, tasting, touching, creating exquisite sensations that were just this side of pain as they sought to give him pleasure.

With a vast effort, Quinn forced himself to remember one final, vital detail. "Jess," he murmured, poised over her. "Is this all right? I don't want you to think I'm the kind of guy who's always prepared, hoping to get lucky, but you did kind of imply. . ."

He was suddenly unreasonably uncomfortable with this entire situation. But the one thing Quinn didn't want to do was give Jessica any reason to be sorry for this in the morning.

It was at that moment, viewing the atypical uncertainty on Quinn's handsome features that Jessica fell totally, irrevocably in love with him. She reached up, running her fingers over his hair, her eyes smiling at him through a sheen of glistening moisture.

"It's all right," she assured him softly.

Knowing how the evening was going to end, she'd seen to that. As much as she wanted Quinn, one thing she didn't need was another child. Especially one born out of wedlock.

"Please, Quinn," she whispered. "Make love to me."

Quinn ceased to think and so did Jessica as they concentrated only on their feelings of shimmering, golden desire. Then he was deep inside her, moving with a fiery strength that fueled their passion until the earth seemed to tilt on its axis, spinning wildly out of control.

AN IMMEASURABLE TIME LATER, Jessica lay in Quinn's arms, content to let the slow, lingering warmth suffuse her languid body. She'd never behaved like that—flinging herself at a man, teasing him, insisting he make love to her—yet she felt not one shred of remorse. Their lovemaking had been the most beautiful thing she'd ever experienced. And although she knew nothing permanent could ever come of it, Jessica refused to allow herself a single regret.

Quinn pressed a light kiss against her temple. "Well, what do you think? Was it the earthquake? Or us?"

"I don't know," she murmured, sighing with sheer pleasure as his fingers trailed down her side. "But I'll bet it registered at least a ten on Richter scales all over the state."

"At least . . . God, you're beautiful."

Her eyes danced as she lifted herself up on one elbow and glanced down at his magnificent, spent body. "So are you."

She watched him laugh, enthralled by the rippling of the muscles of his abdomen. "Men aren't beautiful."

"You are," she insisted. "The most beautiful man I've ever known."

"Known a great many, have you?"

"Jealous?" She grinned down at him. "I'm not asking about the legions of women in your life," she pointed out, not willing to admit he'd only been the second man she'd ever gone to bed with. Why point out her inexperience?

"Ask away," Quinn invited, rolling over, covering her body with his. Jessica thrilled at the feel of his lightly haired legs between hers and gasped as he lowered his head, capturing an ultrasensitive nipple between his lips. "It wouldn't matter, because you're the only one who's ever counted, Jess."

His eyes met hers, and Jessica could not mistake the message she read in their emerald depths. She knew that any other woman would be in seventh heaven to be in her position right now. Figuratively and, she admitted, as his hips rubbed intimately against hers, literally. Quinn hadn't promised her forever, but it was there, gleaming in his tender gaze. Instead of thrilling her, as it once might have, Jessica found the idea of permanency unreasonably frightening.

Conflicting emotions tore at her, drawing her into a vortex of feelings so deep, so overwhelming, that she did not want to think about them any longer. Not tonight.

She nodded, moved beyond words at the love shining in Quinn's wonderful eyes and gave herself up to his tender, intoxicating kiss.

IF JESSICA EXPECTED the magic to disappear with the morning light, she was to be proved wrong. Quinn had infiltrated all the little pockets of her life, and although a part of her remained convinced that this golden-tinged pleasure would soon fade as the following days melted into weeks, Jessica found herself unable to consider a life before him.

They celebrated the Cherry Blossom Festival together, Mallory's camera never ceasing as she filmed the colorfully costumed dancers and floats winding their way through the streets to the graceful Peace Pagoda. Jessica had been attending the annual spring fete since its inception, but never had she enjoyed herself as she did this year.

A San Francisco native, Jessica could be faulted for foregoing the tourist attractions of her beloved city. But as she shared the warm, yellow sunshine of spring with Quinn, she wondered why she had never realized how romantic it could be to walk along Fisherman's Wharf, the pungent aroma of fresh crab and shrimp cooking in sidewalk caldrons mixing enticingly with the tangy sea breezes.

One mellow Sunday afternoon she bought everyone bright, fanciful kites at Ghirardelli Square, and at the end of the day whimsically released hers, watching it disappear into the ruby-and -gold sky over the bay. When Quinn came out of one of the gift shops with a delicate hand-scrolled Victorian locket, Jessica protested at the price, but he refused to listen.

"It's the perfect adornment for a lady aristocrat who possesses the heart of a naughty milkmaid," he murmured for her ears alone, fastening the sterling silver heart about her neck.

Jill decided that it was the most romantic present she'd ever seen. Sara, ever practical, pointed out that the silver was going to need regular polishing. Mallory's camera just whirred away, going in for a tight shot as Quinn's lips grazed Jessica's earlobe.

Quinn was aghast that Jessica had never taken her daughters on a bay tour, insisting they hadn't seen the city until they'd viewed the towering skyline from the water. In order to remedy that situation, he showed up one Saturday morning with tickets for the Blue and Gold cruise. Jill spent the better part of the afternoon seasick from the choppy water, Mallory and Sara argued incessantly over whose fault it was that the bag containing extra videotape cassettes fell overboard into the icy water off the shores of Alcatraz. Jessica ended the day windblown, cold, but unreasonably happy.

Mother Nature seemed determined to bestow upon San Francisco the warmest spring on record, and one balmy day on her lunch hour, Quinn took Jessica to a "brown bag" opera under the branches of the gnarled olive trees in the courtyard of the Cannery. It didn't matter that she couldn't understand the Italian lyrics and was unable to follow the complex drama being played out before her. Because all her attention remained riveted on Quinn, on his every word, his every movement.

Jessica was still floating on a rosy cloud when she returned to the office, and when her intercom buzzed late in the afternoon, she answered it with a feeling of optimism. That feeling quickly disintegrated when a noncommittal Paula stated that Sylvia Thacker was waiting in the reception area.

"Send her in," Jessica instructed, taking a deep breath.

A moment later, a tall, expensively dressed woman marched into the room, settling regally into a chair across from Jessica's desk. Her ash-blond hair was professionally streaked, her makeup impeccable. Only the fire raging in her hazel eyes and the red spots high on her cheeks displayed her aggravation.

"He's done it this time! First, I want him fired. Then we're going to put that bastard in jail. For the rest of his natural life!"

"What did Mr. Thacker do this time?" Jessica asked calmly.

Sylvia reached into her alligator purse, pulling out a handful of newspaper scraps that she dumped unceremoniously on Jessica's desk.

"Look at that!" she instructed.

Jessica smoothed the pieces of newsprint with her hands, fitting the torn scraps into what was obviously the editorial page of the *San Francisco Star*. Her attention was drawn to a skillfully crafted cartoon depicting the incarceration of a local politician for graft.

"I'm afraid I don't understand," Jessica stated, unable to see what it was about the cartoon that had Sylvia so distraught.

A perfectly manicured nail jabbed at the number printed across the politician's striped prison suit. "Does that number ring a bell?" Sylvia inquired caustically.

Jessica stared, then couldn't stop a slight laugh from breaking free. "Oh, my God, that's your phone number!"

Sylvia was on her feet, glaring down at the shredded cartoon with such fire in her eyes that Jessica was surprised it didn't burst into flames.

"Do you have any idea how many weirdos have called me today because of that cartoon? I never realized so many perverts read the editorial pages!" Sylvia wrung her hands and began to pace the floor. "The phone hasn't stopped ringing! You have to do something!" she insisted on a wail that was in direct contrast to her sleek, sophisticated appearance.

"I'll contact Mr. Masterson right away," Jessica promised. "In the meantime, I suppose you should call the telephone company and have your number changed."

"I've already done that. But do you have any idea how many notes I'm going to have to send out letting all my friends know my new number?"

"A Herculean task, at best," Jessica replied dryly.

The slight sarcasm flew right over Sylvia Thacker's head. "It'll take the entire weekend," she agreed. "I want Keith billed for my time that he's wasted," she decided. "After all, I had plans to go to Big Sur. Now I'm going to be stuck at home."

"That is a shame," Jessica said, pressing her luck a bit further. "I take it you don't want to press charges?"

Sylvia looked at Jessica as if she'd just grown an extra head. "Of course I do!"

"May I point out that it will be a bit difficult for Mr. Thacker to pay you restitution if he's locked away in a jail cell? We've already frozen all his liquid assets."

"You have a point," Sylvia agreed thoughtfully. Then her face lit up. "So we'll get him fired. Then we'll take the bastard for all his unemployment!"

Her mood lifted by that idea, Sylvia left the office, chuckling wickedly to herself.

Paula suddenly appeared in the doorway. "Ain't love grand?" she asked with a laugh.

Jessica returned her grin, shaking her head with good-humored frustration. "Would you get me Mr. Masterson?"

"He's on hold now," Paula informed her, reminding Jessica once again how fortunate she was to have such a level-headed secretary. There were times when the woman seemed to read her mind.

"Quinn, we've got a problem," Jessica said as she picked up the receiver.

"I know," he answered immediately. "After such a delightful lunch hour, I can't keep my mind on my work, either. The sun is shining, the birds are singing and I have this irresistible urge to be with my lady.... Let's go sailing," he coaxed. "Then we'll spend the rest of the afternoon and evening making love."

"Quinn," Jessica stated firmly. "This is serious."

"So are my feelings about you, Jess."

There was a suddenly solemn note in his voice that Jessica decided would be best ignored for now. "Sylvia Thacker just left my office and believe me, the woman is looking for blood."

Jessica could hear Quinn's loud sigh. "What happened now?"

"Do you have a copy of this morning's *Star*?"

"Yeah, but it was such a madhouse around here this morning I didn't get a chance to read it. Why?"

"Check out the editorial cartoon," Jessica suggested.

"Just a minute." She could hear Quinn riffling through the newspaper. His roar of laughter indicated he'd just found Keith's latest artistic effort.

"It's not that funny," Jessica insisted sternly, a rebellious chuckle slipping out despite her efforts to remain totally professional.

"No," he agreed, his voice strained as he made a valiant attempt to match her serious tone. "Keith should be ashamed of himself. I suppose she's gotten a few calls."

"The phone hasn't stopped ringing," Jessica informed him.

"I'd better talk with him," Quinn said without a great deal of enthusiasm.

"You do that," Jessica advised dryly. Then she asked a question that had been bothering her from the beginning. "I know why I was stuck with Sylvia's case," she said, remembering Vanessa's explanation. "But for the life of me, I can't figure out why you're putting up with this circus."

"Keith and I were fraternity brothers at USC," Quinn revealed. "One semester I made the mistake of taking an art history class. Since I seem to lack the ability to tell a Rembrandt from a Matisse, I was in real trouble. Then to top it all off, I got mono.

"Keith showed up at the infirmary every day, drilling me on paintings until I knew enough to get a respectable C on the makeup final."

"So you're paying him back by handling his divorce?"

"He's not such a bad guy when he's off the booze. And you can't deny the fact that he's a genius at what he does."

"If he doesn't stop drinking," Jessica suggested, "he's going to be submitting those cartoons from a jail cell."

"I'll talk to him," Quinn promised. "And, Jess?" His tone suddenly deepened.

"Yes?"

"Have a good day."

Such simple words, she considered. She heard them continually from salesclerks, bus drivers, strangers. So why did they cause her heartbeat to quicken?

"Thank you," she murmured. "You too."

"I intend to," he agreed on a thick, sensual rumble. "I'm going to spend the day thinking of you."

The smile remained on Jessica's face long after she'd hung up. What a difference Quinn had made in her life, she thought as she returned to work.

As SPRING BLOSSOMED, every day seemed unnaturally special, every moment delightfully memorable, and if Jessica ever suffered doubts about the fragile foundations of their affair, she pushed them to a far corner of her mind.

Her daughters took Quinn's presence in stride, and although they'd dropped more than one heavy hint that Jessica wasn't getting any younger, they wisely refrained from mentioning marriage. It was obvious, however, that they adored him.

Based on what Elizabeth was willing to state about Mac's impetuous trip to Monterey, Jessica determined that her father had made the mistake of demanding that his wife return with him. Now Elizabeth seemed bent on teaching him a lesson, and after forty-six years of marriage, Mac was forced to court his wife all over again. From those nights that Elizabeth didn't return home after a theater date, Jessica could only surmise that things were looking up on the MacLaughlin home front.

They'd been together six weeks when Quinn's patience ground to a halt. Except for those times that Elizabeth was out of town, or staying with Mac, and Jessica's daughters were in Marin County with Brian O'Neill, he and Jessica would make love at his apartment, forcing him to drive her home in the cold, lonely predawn hours.

"I want to stay with you all night," he complained as the car idled outside her house. "I want to hold you in my arms when we go to sleep and wake up with you in the morning."

"We will," she promised. "This weekend."

"Dammit, Jess," he argued, banging his fist on the steering wheel, "it's not enough! I'm tired of receiving bits and pieces of you. I want to be an integral part of your life. I want to know I'm important to you."

She framed his face with her hands, pressing a soft kiss against his tight lips. "You are important to me, Quinn," she murmured.

"Then let's live together," he suggested, as if the thought had just occurred to him. In truth, he'd been waiting days for the right moment. It was now or never, he decided.

She dropped her hands, shaking her head sadly. "You know I can't do that, darling. Not with the girls. It wouldn't be a good influence."

"What if you didn't have the girls?" he pressed, believing Jessica's objections to deepening their relationship went further than she was willing to admit.

"Are you suggesting I send them to live with Brian?"

Quinn hastened to dispel her misconception. "Of course not. It was just a hypothetical question. If it were only the two of us involved, would you live with me?"

Jessica wanted to say yes, that were it not for their situation, she would open her house, her heart, her life to him unconditionally. But in all honesty, she knew that wasn't entirely true. She was happy enough with the way things were right now. Granted, her bed seemed unreasonably lonely when she crawled between the cold sheets while the world still lay shrouded in darkness. And there were times when she'd look up to say something to Quinn, only to realize he wasn't there. He was across town, in his own apartment.

But those were only minor inconveniences compared to the problems they'd have if they were living together. Separate but equal. That was the new Jessica O'Neill motto.

"That's a moot point," she said, finally answering Quinn's question. "I'm the mother of three impressionable daughters. You knew that when you entered into this affair, Quinn."

It was at that moment Quinn decided he'd better leave before he said something he'd regret.

"You're right," he agreed without a great deal of enthusiasm, getting out of the car to walk her to the door. "I'll just have to work around the barriers."

Jessica didn't know exactly what Quinn meant by that vague statement, but she didn't like the glint of determination in his green eyes or the firm thrust of his jaw as he gave her an unusually circumspect good-night kiss. His odd behavior created a sense of foreboding that stayed with her the remainder of the night, making sleep an impossibility.

9

JESSICA'S FEARS WERE REALIZED as she entered the kitchen the next morning to find Quinn seated comfortably at the breakfast table, his long fingers wrapped around a mug of steaming coffee. At any other time, the sight of him would have given her a lift, but she was still unnerved by the intensity of his demands last night. Also, the expectant expressions on the faces of her mother and daughters made Jessica immediately suspicious. She couldn't forget his softly veiled threat about working around the barriers.

"What are you doing here?"

"Good morning to you, too," he stated with a smile.

Jessica let out an annoyed breath. She was due in court in two hours, she was exhausted before the day had even begun thanks to worrying about Quinn all night, and some maniac with a jackhammer was banging away in her head. She was in no mood to be gracious.

"Dammit, I asked you a question, Quinn."

"Jessica!" Elizabeth MacLaughlin turned from the stove, staring in disbelief at her daughter's blatant rudeness.

"Don't worry about it." Quinn sent her mother a broad grin. "I've already discovered our Jessie's not a morning person."

"That's for sure," Mallory offered helpfully, her camera directed toward the action being played out before her. "Mom won't talk to anyone until she's had her coffee."

"Well, we can't expect her to be perfect," Quinn remarked casually, rising from the table to pour some coffee into a bright mug.

"Here you go, darling," he said, leaning down to give her a peck on the cheek. "Drink up." He pulled out a chair for her.

"What are you doing here?" she tried for a third time, taking the chair he offered. She turned to her middle daughter. "Mallory, I'm in no mood for your project this morning!"

"You're going to want this saved for posterity," Mallory answered, zooming in for a close-up.

"I don't like the sound of this," Jessica groaned. "What am I going to want saved?"

"We've been planning your wedding," Quinn announced blandly.

Jessica choked on her coffee at the casual way he'd just dropped his bombshell. "Wedding?" she managed to gasp finally.

Quinn handed her a paper napkin. "Wedding," he repeated.

"It's going to be the most romantic wedding ever," Jill said on a deep sigh.

"You're going to love it," Sara agreed, bobbing her bright head. "Even Gran is all for it."

Quinn nodded. "Your mother had an elaborate church wedding in mind, but knowing how you're really a romantic at heart, I thought you might prefer the Japanese Tea Gardens. . . . I can picture you in that ivory lace dress you wore to George and Gloria's anniversary party, cherry blossoms woven through your lush auburn waves."

He glanced disparagingly at the elaborate twist he'd made at the back of her neck. "You'll wear your hair down, of course, instead of tying it up like some old maid schoolteacher."

Elizabeth forestalled Jessica's furious response as she set a plate of scorched bacon and runny eggs before Quinn, then placed an identical breakfast in front of Jessica, her stern look indicating she expected her daughter to eat it.

Jessica ignored the food. "Exactly who am I supposed to be marrying?"

"Why, Quinn, of course." Elizabeth laughed. "We should be hurt that you didn't tell us about all this sooner, Jessica. But he explained that you'd wanted to give the girls a chance to get used to him before breaking the news."

"We think it's terrific, Mom," Mallory enthused.

"Absolutely awesome," Jill agreed.

"And about time," Sara said, adding her two cents. "It's not healthy for a woman your age to be living alone."

Jessica shot her daughters a warning glance. "If I want any remarks from the peanut gallery, I'll ask for them," she snapped. "And, Mallory, for the last time, put that camera down or you won't get any allowance for the next twenty years!"

Then, if looks could kill, the one Jessica gave Quinn would have put him six feet under. The girls shifted nervously in their seats, and Mallory reluctantly lowered her camera. Only Elizabeth remained blissfully unaware of Jessica's exacerbation.

"I have to admit, dear," she trilled merrily, "that when Quinn first brought up the subject of having the wedding at the gardens, I found it rather avant-garde. But once he started describing the flowers, your dress and the strolling minstrels, I decided it was a delightful idea."

"Thank you, Lizzie." Quinn grinned up at Elizabeth, who smiled back.

"Lizzie?" Jessica arched a tawny brow. Her mother was a stickler for formality, she couldn't imagine anyone daring to use that nickname on Elizabeth MacLaughlin.

"Quinn decided that calling Gran Elizabeth would be too stuffy, once you were married," Mallory explained.

"And I'd feel absolutely ancient having a handsome man like Quinn call me Mother," Elizabeth interjected.

"Especially since no one would ever believe you were old enough," Quinn said smoothly, directing an appreciative smile Elizabeth's way.

Jessica stared as her mother giggled like an adolescent schoolgirl. "Quinn came up with Lizzie, and after trying it out a few times, I think I like it."

"We have to talk," Jessica said sternly, glaring across the table at the irritatingly smug man.

"Uh-oh," Jill said. "I think I'm going to be late for school."

"Me too!" Mallory exclaimed, jumping up from the table.

"Wait for me!" Sara appeared as eager as her sisters to escape from the room. "Have a good day, Mom," she called back over her shoulder. "Good luck, Quinn!"

"Of course we'll discuss everything in detail, darling," Quinn agreed readily, waving goodbye to Jessica's daughters as they scurried out the door. "Have you chosen a spot for our honeymoon yet?"

"There's not going to be any honeymoon!"

"Sure there is," he corrected smoothly, eyeing her wickedly over the rim of his mug. "You don't think I'd forego that pleasure, do you? I know we both have our work, Jess, but all it'll take is a little juggling of schedules."

"I'm not juggling my schedule for you, Quinn Masterson, so get that idea out of your head. And I'm not going on a honeymoon with you, because I'm not marrying you. We had an agreement and you've no right to go changing the rules!" She was on her feet, glaring down at him, her eyes ablaze.

"If you young people are going to argue," Elizabeth murmured calmly, "I think I'll go upstairs to watch 'Wheel of Fortune' on the bedroom television." She turned in the doorway. "Speaking of bedrooms, dear, if you both decide to live here, I'd better bring home some new fabric swatches. That floral print is far too feminine for a man like Quinn."

Jessica watched her mother leave, then spun toward Quinn. "You had absolutely no right to do that!"

Quinn took his time answering, biting off a piece of black bacon. "You know, this stuff isn't so bad once you get used to it. I just realized we've been eating out so much that I never asked if you inherited your mother's culinary skills. Not that I mind continuing to eat in restaurants," he assured her with a broad smile. "Home cooking is highly overrated."

A wry glance down at his plate seconded that opinion. "Of course, there's something to be said for being greeted at the door by an adoring wife, clad in a frilly little pink apron," he mused aloud. "Have I ever told you my fantasy about—"

"Why did you do that?" she interrupted sharply.

His expression was blissfully innocent. "Do what?"

"Let my family think we're getting married. What do you suggest we do when they find out it's a lie?"

"What makes you think it's a lie?" He rose abruptly, carrying his plate to the sink where he rinsed it and placed it in the dishwasher. Then he looked back over his shoulder. "Are you going to eat that?"

"You know I don't eat breakfast."

He shook his head. "For an intelligent woman, you sure do have a lot of bad habits. You're stubborn, you steal the blankets on the rare occasion we do manage to spend an entire night together, you're a washout at plane geometry and you've got lousy nutritional habits, as well. . . . It's amazing that you were able to land yourself such a terrific catch." His grin only served to irritate Jessica further.

"It damn well *is* a lie and you know it!"

Quinn didn't answer immediately. Instead he dumped her untouched food into the disposal and finished clearing the table. Jessica's irritation rose even higher as he filled the dishwasher with detergent and turned it on, wiping the counter off with a wet sponge.

She marched over to him, grabbing his arm to turn him toward her. "Would you have the common courtesy to discuss this rationally? I love my children and I'm not going to let some louse hurt them!"

"That's a rotten thing to call your fiancé, Jessica," he said, shaking his head sadly.

"Knock it off, Quinn," she snapped. "This isn't funny."

To her amazement, his expression was suddenly unnervingly solemn. "I never meant it to be. I've been thinking about us a lot lately, Jess, and I've come to the conclusion that I'm sick and tired of this damn affair you've got us locked into."

"Oh."

Jessica turned around, struggling for composure, damned if she was going to let him see her cry. Well, here it was, the goodbye she'd been waiting for. So why did she suddenly feel as if he'd knocked every bit of breath from her body?

Quinn reached out, shaping her shoulders with his hands, the gesture both soothing and possessive. "It isn't what you think," he murmured, his lips grazing the soft skin of her neck. "This arrangement is ridiculous. I love you. I want to marry you. This afternoon couldn't be fast enough, but I'm willing to wait until you can make whatever arrangements women make at a time like this."

She shook her head. "I'm not marrying you, Quinn. I told you that from the beginning."

"*In* the beginning," he corrected calmly. "Before you knew how perfect I was for you. How perfect we were for each other."

"Why are you doing this?" she asked weakly, moving out of his grasp, turning to face him.

"Why do you think?"

Her mind whirled into gear, latching onto the first possible answer. Although she was inclined to disregard the outrageous idea, she couldn't forget the fact that Quinn could not be taken lightly as an adversary.

"We're not going to drop the suit against Keith for printing that cartoon," she warned. "I'm honestly sorry he was fired from the paper, but you have to admit he deserved it."

A nerve twitched along his tight jaw. "Dammit, Jessica, if you think I give two hoots in hell about that crazy couple, you're mistaken. Besides, there isn't going to be any divorce."

"What do you know that I don't?" she asked archly.

"Nothing, really. But this is the fifth time in the past four years Sylvia has sued Keith for divorce. She didn't go through with it any of the other times."

"But she seems to hate him."

"That's right," he agreed. "And at the moment, the guy isn't too fond of her, either. But what we have here is a couple of fruitcakes who can't live with each other, or without each other, either."

"This could always be the time she sticks to her guns," Jessica argued.

"Could be," he said. "But I don't want to talk about them, Jess. It's time we discussed us. We've been sidestepping this issue for weeks. Give me one good reason why we shouldn't get married."

"I don't love you," she lied through her teeth.

Keep it light, Quinn tried to warn himself, realizing that he'd misjudged Jessica's aversion to marriage. The one thing he hadn't wanted to do was box her into a corner. But he'd used up his store of patience; he didn't want to continue living in this limbo she'd made of their relationship.

Jessica didn't like the way Quinn just stood there, eyeing her thoughtfully.

"What now?" she asked finally, unable to bear the stifling silence any longer.

"Your nose," he murmured.

"What about my nose?"

"I was wondering if it grew when you told these big whoppers." He paused, his gaze intent. "I guess not," he said a second later. "It's just as well. I'm particularly fond of the cute little ski-jump effect at the end." He ran his finger along the slightly upward tilt. "It's downright adorable."

Jessica scowled up at him, refusing to answer that ridiculous statement.

"You know," he went on, "Lizzie's a real nice lady, and I've always respected and admired the judge, but I think your parents spoiled you. They probably should have spanked you from time to time. To keep you more manageable."

Jessica could read the gleam in his eyes as easily as a child's primer. "Don't even suggest it," she warned.

He flung his hand over his chest, looking astonished and a little hurt. "Me? Why, Jessie, I'd never dare suggest such a thing." Then he grinned. "The idea does have a few intriguing aspects, though."

It was the smile more than anything that broke the last fragile thread of her self-restraint. She couldn't bear the thought that Quinn considered this, the most important conversation she'd ever had in her life, nothing but a joke.

"I don't love you," she repeated firmly.

Her softly spoken words tore at Quinn and he tried to think of something, anything, to say that would change the course of events.

"You don't mean that."

It was the hardest thing Jessica had ever done, but the pain she thought she'd overcome returned from the past, reminding her that if she gave in to Quinn on this, she'd find herself right back where she'd started. Quinn was a wonderful man.

But he was strong willed, as well. How long would he allow her the freedom to make her own choices? To be her own woman?

His behavior today, springing this news on her family, was proof that if she married him, she'd end up living her life under his rules. He hadn't asked her to marry him—he'd insisted as if it were a foregone conclusion.

She swallowed, having to push the words past the lump in her throat. "I do," she whispered.

Quinn flinched visibly. "Well," he said, "I guess since I don't want an affair and you don't want marriage, we've just reached an impasse."

She turned away, unable to bear the pain she viewed darkening his gentle green eyes. "I suppose so."

A stifling silence settled over them, like a morning fog that had yet to burn off.

"Then this is goodbye?"

She nodded, unable to answer.

Quinn didn't want to accept the fact that this was happening. He didn't want to believe Jessica could throw everything away, just to stick to her ridiculous principles that no longer had any bearing on who they were. Or what they had together.

"You're going to end it, aren't you? After all we've had." His ragged tone displayed his own grief and disbelief at the way things had turned out.

Tears welled up in her eyes, but she didn't dare turn around, knowing that if she looked at him, she'd recant her earlier statement. She wanted him. She wanted to be with him. Why couldn't he just leave things as they were?

His frustration finally reaching the boiling point, Quinn turned on his heel, marching out the door before he gave in to instinct and drove his fist through the sunshine yellow wall. The screen door broke off its hinges as he slammed it behind him, causing Jessica's copper gelatin molds to fall off the wall. She stared out into the slanting rain, watching him drive away. And then she cried.

TEN DAYS DRAGGED BY without a word from Quinn. Ten very long days and even longer sleepless nights. Jessica attempted to keep her mind on her work, but she felt like a walking zombie as she made a series of foolish, unthinking mistakes that had her spending an uncomfortable amount of time in George Bennington's office.

She had finally made it through her first year at the firm, but Jessica knew she still was on probation. Despite his friendship with her father, the head of the law firm believed in trial by fire. Jessica decided if George Bennington told her one more time that if she couldn't stand the heat, she had better get out of the kitchen, she would save him the trouble of firing her and quit. She'd had several meetings with the District Attorney, and his offer was looking better every day.

Keith Thacker seemed to have dropped off the face of the earth, and Sylvia called several times each day, distraught that Jessica could not locate her missing husband. Continual telephone calls to Quinn's office to inquire about his errant client proved fruitless. His secretary steadfastly insisted that Quinn was out of town on business and although she dutifully accepted Jessica's messages, Quinn seemed determined to ignore her calls.

Things were no better at home. While she was in the throes of editing her project, Mallory's unusual displays of temper flared out of control at the slightest provocation. Every evening Jessica was forced to watch the latest version, her heart aching as she viewed flashbacks of those happy, seemingly carefree days she'd spent with Quinn.

Sara was unusually quiet, but had brought home a note from her teacher, stating that the straight A student was in danger of failing both English composition and math and might be held back unless her grades showed a marked improvement in the next month.

Jill, whose punk rock style had always left a great deal to be desired, came home from spending the night with a new friend, her hair dyed a brilliant fluorescent green and a trio of holes pierced in each earlobe.

Jessica knew her daughters blamed her for Quinn's disappearance from their lives, a fact she could not deny. She also suspected that their uncharacteristic behavior was a direct result of her break with him, but there was little she could do to change things, even if she wanted to. Like his client, Quinn appeared to have vanished.

The only bright spot in her life came when Elizabeth returned to the house late one afternoon, Mac in tow.

"Jessica," her father's booming voice greeted her, "I'm glad you're home. Your mother and I have some good news!"

"I could use some," Jessica muttered, looking up from the brief she was preparing. Then her glance sharpened. Were her parents actually holding hands? "Mother's moved back home," she guessed.

"Nope. Well, that, too." Her father's blue eyes danced with merriment. "But we've even something more exciting to tell you."

"What's going on?"

"We've just put a down payment on a lovely sailboat, dear," her mother broke in.

"A sailboat?"

"A sailboat," Mac confirmed. "We're sailing around the world together. Just the two of us." He smiled down at Elizabeth, whose own gaze was brimming with affection as she grinned back.

"That's the most ridiculous idea you've come up with yet," Jessica snapped waspishly, feeling unreasonably irritated by the warm and loving looks her parents were exchanging.

She had wanted her parents to work out their problems, really she did. So why did their news make her feel even worse? There was only one answer, and Jessica hated to even consider it. She was jealous! Of her own parents.

"We used to sail every weekend, before we both got too wrapped up in our work to take the time," Elizabeth countered. "We know what we're doing."

"I don't remember sailing," Jessica muttered.

"Of course not, Jessica," her father said with the tone of consummate logic he'd used for years on the bench. "Since we gave it up before you were born, you couldn't possibly recall the fun we used to have."

"Well, I only hope you both know what you're doing," she stated on a resigned sigh.

Her parents exchanged a long look. Then Mac nodded at Elizabeth, who took a deep breath and delicately brought up the subject everyone had been tiptoeing around lately.

"We do," she agreed. "But we have to wonder if you know what you're doing, dear."

"I suppose you're talking about Quinn," she said heavily. Jessica had no desire to discuss the topic of her breakup with anyone. Even her parents. Especially her parents.

"Hell's bells, Jessie," Mac broke in. "Anyone could tell the man was head over heels in love with you. And your mother said you felt the same way about him. So what's the problem?"

"It's too complicated to explain," Jessica said, neatly sidestepping the issue, returning her attention to her work.

"You should have been firmer with Jessica when she was young, Mac," Elizabeth pointed out. "This is all your fault."

"My fault?" Mac blustered. "You were the one in charge of discipline, my dear. Besides, she certainly didn't inherit this stubborn trait from me!"

Elizabeth stiffened. "Well, don't blame me. Everyone knows the MacLaughlins have a stubborn streak a mile wide."

"And the Cunninghams don't?" he asked incredulously. "You haven't exactly been a model of compliancy all these years, yourself, Elizabeth. You're every bit as ornery as your mother!"

Elizabeth bristled. "I thought you liked my mother!"

"I never said I didn't like her," he countered brusquely. "I simply pointed out that Marion Cunningham was every bit as unbending as her daughter." His accusing glare shifted from Elizabeth to Jessica. "And her granddaughter."

"You two are going to be alone together on a boat for months and months?" Jessica questioned dryly. "It'll be interesting to see who throws who overboard first."

"Your mother and I understand each other," Mac stated firmly. "Which is more than I can say for you and Quinn."

"I don't want to talk about him," Jessica insisted.

"Just like a Cunningham," Mac muttered, raking his fingers through his silver hair.

"Just like a MacLaughlin," Elizabeth commented at the same time.

They both looked at each other and laughed.

"Look, honey," Elizabeth began again, trying reason. "It's only going to take a month to get the boat seaworthy—"

"Don't forget repainted," Mac cut in.

Elizabeth's smile was beatific. "She's named the *Sea Hawk*, right now," she explained to Jessica. "Mac's rechristening her the *Elizabeth*."

"That's nice," Jessica admitted.

"Isn't it?" Elizabeth agreed, momentarily sidetracked.

"So you see, Jessie—" Mac picked up the conversational ball "—we're only going to be in town another month, but there's still plenty of time to have that wedding in the Japanese Tea Gardens."

"How did you know about that?"

"I told him," Elizabeth stated. "And I still think it's a lovely idea, Jessica."

"There isn't going to be any wedding," Jessica insisted firmly. "Besides, even if I changed my mind, I haven't heard a word from Quinn in almost two weeks. He's obviously lost interest."

Frustration was etched onto every line of both her parents' faces, but knowing their daughter as well as they did, both shook their heads, giving up for the time being on convincing her of her folly.

10

THREE WEEKS AFTER HER FIGHT with Quinn, Jessica was doodling idly on a yellow legal pad one morning, her mind wandering as she attempted to come up with one good reason why she should stay in her office. She was unreasonably restless. At one time, her work at Bennington, Marston, White and Lowell had been the most important thing in her life—next to her daughters, of course.

But she was slowly discovering that the world of corporate law was as dry as the legal briefs she slaved over all day. The only truly interesting case she'd had in months had been the Thackers' divorce case. While Sylvia and Keith Thacker's behavior had been admittedly frustrating, at least it offered some drama. Unfortunately, she mused, gazing absently out the window, with Keith apparently out of the city, the marital wars had settled into a period of cease-fire, so she didn't even have the battling Thackers to take her mind off Quinn.

"I hope that look isn't directed at anyone I know."

Jessica glanced up to see Vanessa standing in the doorway. "No. Just the world in general."

"Bad day?"

"Bad year."

"The only thing I know that'll put me in the dumps as low as you seem to be is man trouble."

Jessica merely shrugged, covering the paper with lopsided stars.

Vanessa came into the room, taking a chair opposite Jessica's desk. "Have you seen Quinn Masterson lately?" she asked with studied carelessness.

Jessica switched to squares. "No." At Vanessa's continuing silence, she glanced up. "Why?"

The woman's gaze circled the room as she suddenly appeared unwilling to meet Jessica's eyes. "Just wondering . . . Pamela Stuart just returned from Mexico."

"That's nice," Jessica murmured, her fingers tightening around the slim gold pen.

"She came back with a nice tan."

Jessica dropped the pen, placed her elbows on the desk and rested her chin on her linked fingers. "You didn't come all the way down the hall to tell me Pamela Stuart has a tan," she accused. "So, what's up?"

Vanessa fiddled nervously with her ring. "She got a divorce down there, Jessica."

"Good for her. There seems to be a lot of that going around these days," Jessica responded dryly.

"There's something else."

"I figured there would be," Jessica agreed on a slight sigh. "Here's where you tell me she was out with Quinn, right?"

"I'm afraid so." Vanessa's brown eyes were filled with consolation.

So that's where he'd been. In Mexico, holding Pamela's hand while she'd gotten her divorce. The thought caused pain to fork through Jessica.

"Not that it matters," Jessica asserted on a feigned, casual note, "but they're just old friends."

"They looked pretty friendly last night, all right," Vanessa stated, her meaning readily apparent.

"I don't want to talk about Pamela Stuart, or Quinn," Jessica said firmly.

Vanessa rose from her chair with a fluid, graceful motion. "Okay," she said companionably. "I just felt you should know. I'd hate to see you hurt, Jessica."

As she left the room, Jessica considered that Vanessa's warning had come too late. She was already hurting more than she'd ever deemed possible. If she'd thought she'd gone through hell when her marriage had broken up, Jessica was discovering she'd been sadly mistaken.

As if conjured up by some fiendish genie of her thought process, Paula announced a few minutes later that Quinn Masterson was holding on the line.

Jessica stared mutely at the blinking red button, eyeing it with the uneasiness one might view a diamondback rattlesnake, poised to strike. *This is ridiculous*, she mentally lashed out at herself, punching the button.

"Hello?" Damn. She'd planned on sounding brisk, efficient. Instead a revealing, soft note had crept into her voice.

Quinn, on the other hand, seemed to have no difficulty in maintaining a curt, professional tone.

"Jessica," he stated without preamble. "I need to know if Sylvia Thacker will agree to a meeting."

"Where on earth has Keith been? Sylvia's been driving me crazy."

"He checked into a detox center in Phoenix."

"Oh. How is he?"

"Better. He's a long way from being a recovered alcoholic, but at least he isn't at rock bottom any longer."

Jessica wished she could say the same for herself. "I'll check with Sylvia and get back to you," she agreed, struggling to match his impersonal tone. "Will you be in your office all afternoon?"

"I've got a lunch appointment that may run a little long. But you can leave a message with my secretary."

Jessica couldn't help wondering if his lunch date was with the newly divorced Pamela Stuart. "Fine," she agreed curtly. "Well, have a good day."

"If I thought you meant that," he muttered, "we just might have something to talk about."

With that inscrutable statement he hung up, leaving the dial tone buzzing in her ear. Shaking her head with frustration, Jessica dialed Sylvia Thacker's number.

"So the little worm wants to crawl back, does he?" the woman asked gleefully.

"I don't really know," Jessica answered. "Mr. Masterson called and informed me that your husband was requesting a meeting. He didn't go into details."

"Well, he's going to have a lot of apologizing to do if he thinks he's getting back in this house!"

"Mrs. Thacker," Jessica pleaded, running out of patience, "shall I set a time or not?"

"I suppose that's okay," the woman stated thoughtfully. "But don't make it right away. Let the squirt squirm for a while, that's what I always say."

"I know," Jessica murmured, wondering what kind of marriage Sylvia and Keith Thacker had that they could fight so furiously, say such terrible things about each other, then put everything aside and reconcile again. Remembering what Quinn had alleged about their past record, she had the feeling that was what was about to happen.

"By the way, what gutter did Masterson find him in this time?" Sylvia asked, as if on an afterthought.

"Your husband was in a detoxification center in Phoenix," Jessica answered briskly.

There was a long silence on the other end of the line. "Are you telling me that Keith managed to dry himself out?"

"Quinn, uh, Mr. Masterson, said he's doing better," Jessica replied noncommittally.

Again, there was a thoughtful pause. "I'll be damned," Sylvia murmured. "See if you can make that appointment for tomorrow," she instructed. "This I have to see."

Jessica agreed, then waited until late in the afternoon to return Quinn's call, unreasonably anxious for another opportunity to speak with him. But his irritatingly professional secretary informed her that Mr. Masterson was still out. However, according to his calendar, tomorrow morning at ten would be fine, the woman confirmed, promising to pass the message on to her employer.

"Burning the midnight oil?" Vanessa paused in the office doorway, regarding Jessica curiously. "Come on, kiddo. It's time to go home."

"I've got some work to finish up," Jessica stated, unwilling to admit she was hoping Quinn might call to confirm the meeting. She hadn't realized until that unsatisfactory conversation this morning how desperately she'd been needing to hear his voice.

"I thought your mother moved back home."

Jessica made a notation in the margin of a study of Marin County demographics she'd been compiling for George Bennington. "She did," she answered absently.

"So who's with the kids?"

"They don't have school tomorrow—a teachers' meeting or something—so they've gone up to Mill Valley to spend the weekend with their father. Mallory finished her movie about the family and wanted to show it to Brian."

"How did it turn out?"

"Terrific," Jessica admitted, hoping that she wasn't revealing how painful it had been to watch the final version of Mallory's ninety-minute videotape last evening. Quinn had been all too evident, and it had been incredibly distressful, watching her life played out before her eyes, a horrible flashback of her latest failure. "She's really very talented."

"You're on your own tonight?"

"I guess so," Jessica agreed glumly.

"Want to go get a drink? The Cosmic Kitten has a dynamite happy hour."

Jessica grimaced. "I've never liked singles' bars. Besides, I've heard that place is a meat market."

"Of course it is," Vanessa concurred. "But at least the meat is prime. And heterosexual, which in this town is a decided plus."

"I think I'll pass."

"You can't sit around here moping over the great Quinn Masterson forever," she advised.

"I'm not moping, I'm working."

Vanessa came into the office, perching on the corner of Jessica's desk, crossing long legs clad in a patterned navy blue hose that exactly matched her silk suit. Jessica wondered idly if other women were born with the ability for coordinating their wardrobes—possessing an extra gene, or chromosome, or something. Whatever, she decided on an audible sigh, she'd obviously been out to lunch when that particular talent was handed out.

"Jessica," Vanessa said firmly, "surviving a broken love affair is like riding a horse. Sure you fall off, but you have to get right back on again."

"I've always been allergic to horses."

"You know what I'm talking about," Vanessa snapped. "The way you've been acting, it's like you're allergic to men. Believe me, honey, it'll do you a world of good to go out and have a little fun. It wouldn't hurt your reputation any, either."

"What does that mean?" Jessica demanded.

Vanessa's perfect white teeth worried her lower lip as she appeared to be making a decision. "Look," she said, "I want you to know I never believed a single word, but people have been talking about you."

"About me?" Jessica couldn't imagine people so bored with their own lives that they'd find her an interesting topic of conversation.

"Well, until that little fling with the Casanova of San Francisco's legal world, you didn't date. Not that anyone could tell."

"I'm amazed that *anyone* bothered to notice," Jessica snapped.

"You have to admit it *is* unusual. After all, you're an attractive woman who happens to be at an age when your sexuality should be at its peak. And you're a divorcée to boot."

Jessica didn't miss the implication. She shook her head with very real irritation. "And therefore I should be hot to trot, right?"

The other woman appeared unperturbed by Jessica's prickly tone. "Well, to be perfectly honest, it's common knowledge that you've turned down dates with just about every single male in the office. And a few of the married ones, as well." Her voice dropped conspiratorially. "Some of the men don't think that's quite natural, if you get my drift."

Jessica got it all right. Loud and clear. Her blue eyes hardened. "My life is my own business, Vanessa. And I intend to keep it that way."

The woman shrugged elegantly, sliding off the desk. "Well," she murmured, "don't say I didn't try to warn you." She turned in the doorway. "Are you sure you won't change your mind about that drink?"

"I'm sure."

"Don't work too hard," she advised, her fingers fluttering goodbye as she turned and left the office.

As Jessica watched Vanessa leave, she couldn't help recalling Quinn's accusation that Jessica O'Neill was rumored to be an iron lady with ice water for blood and a stone heart. A lot they all knew. Jessica considered how lucky she'd be if that was only true. After all, stone hearts were probably incapable of breaking.

Much later, Jessica stood at her office window. Even through the thick glass she could hear the lonely whine of a siren and glanced down toward the street, where the car lights glowed like stars that had fallen to the ground.

"Excuse me?"

She turned to look at the woman who stood hesitantly in the doorway, a vacuum in one hand and a tray filled with cans of spray polish, dust rags and Windex in the other.

"Is it all right if I clean in here now?"

Jessica took one last look at the telephone, willing it to ring. Then, admitting that Quinn had no intention of calling, she gave the waiting woman an apologetic smile.

"I'm on my way out," she said, taking her purse from a bottom drawer. "I'm sorry I held you up."

"No bother. Have a nice night," the woman called after her.

"You too," she answered automatically.

As Jessica sat gazing out the window on the bus home, she decided that everyone in San Francisco was out taking Vanessa's advice. The sidewalks were crowded with throngs of happy couples, holding hands, laughing, seemingly having a wonderful time. When the bus halted at a stoplight, a couple in a convertible beside her exchanged a brief, but unmistakedly heated kiss. San Francisco might be the city for lovers, but this evening Jessica found all that romance most depressing.

When she finally arrived home, Jessica decided that she deserved a little pampering. She filled the tub to the rim with hot water, dumping in an outrageously expensive amount of bath oil. Then she dug out a novel she'd been intending to read for months and poured a glass of wine. Reconsidering, she retrieved the bottle from the refrigerator, taking it into the bathroom with her.

Although Jessica's mind wandered, as it did continually these days to Quinn, she forced her attention back to the story, letting some of the cool water out of the tub, refilling it as needed. She'd managed to make it to the third chapter when the lights flickered once. Then twice. Then went out altogether.

"Damn," she muttered, rising from the tub and grabbing for a towel in the dark. Wrapping it about herself she went into the kitchen, taking a candle from the cache she kept for just this reason.

"I'll be glad when that electrician is finished," she said under her breath, digging around in the drawer where she stored the spare fuses.

Jessica made her way by the flickering, dim candlelight to the fuse box located on the back porch. She replaced one, but nothing happened. Muttering a series of low oaths that would have drawn an arched eyebrow even from the often colorful Judge MacLaughlin, she returned to the kitchen, taking her last replacement fuse from the drawer.

"This better do the trick," Jessica grumbled. "Because I'm in no mood to spend the night reading by candlelight."

She held her breath, and was rewarded as the house once again glowed with light. "Bingo," she stated, pleased that something, at least, had worked out well for her today. Even though Jessica didn't believe in omens, a little corner of her mind latched on to this good fortune as a hopeful sign.

That slim vestige of hope began to dissolve as she awoke the next morning twenty minutes late, having forgotten to reset her clock radio after the power had gone out. Her hair dryer blew yet another fuse before she'd finished, and as she viewed her wild tangle of wet auburn hair in the mirror, Jessica considered how on the one day she wanted to look her best, she was going to show up for her meeting with Quinn looking like a drowned rat.

Her day continued its downhill slide on the way to the office. The bus driver slammed on his brakes, narrowly avoiding hitting a child who'd run into the street, chasing a baseball thrown to him by a companion. The violent motion sent coffee splashing out of the paper cup held by the passenger next to Jessica, and she watched fatalistically as the dark liquid spread all over the skirt of her blue shirtwaist dress.

"I'm sorry," the distraught commuter moaned, dabbing ineffectually at her skirt with his handkerchief.

"Don't worry about it," Jessica said on a slight sigh. "You couldn't help it."

"But your dress. Look, send me the bill and I'll pay for the cleaning, all right?"

"Really—"

"It's the least I can do," he insisted.

Jessica took the business card he offered, slipping it into her purse. She had no intention of contacting the man again. It wasn't his fault. She was rapidly coming to the conclusion that some fiendishly evil being had taken control of the universe, manipulating events so that anything that might possibly go wrong would. This individual was simply a pawn in the game being played with her life.

The Thackers were waiting for her, as was Quinn, and all heads turned expectantly to the door as she entered. Jessica's heart sank as Quinn's eyes narrowed, taking in her disheveled appearance, but she straightened her shoulders determinedly and entered the room with a false, professional smile.

"I'm sorry I'm late," she stated, taking a seat beside Sylvia Thacker at the conference table. "My alarm clock went off late. You see, I blew two fuses last night, and another this morning, and . . . Well, you don't care about that." She managed another brilliant smile. "Shall we get started? Who wants to go first?"

I'm babbling, Jessica groaned inwardly. *They're all going to think I'm an absolute idiot.* She risked a glance at Quinn, her heart sinking further as she viewed his incredulous gaze.

But Quinn was not listening to Jessica's breathless statement; indeed, her words were a distant hum, hardly audible over the blood roaring in his ears. She'd changed amazingly in the past few weeks. Her face was thinner, paler. A sprinkling of freckles that hadn't been visible before stood out on her cheekbones. Her eyes were bright with nervousness, but it would be impossible to miss the deep purple shadows underneath them. And while he was no authority on women's bodies, he knew Jessica's intimately. How many pounds had she lost? Five? Ten? She looked, in all honesty, as bad as he felt. But she still looked wonderful.

Jessica had been hoping that they could get right down to business, but it appeared the Thackers had their own ideas. Each proceeded to voice a litany of complaints against the other, point and counterpoint, back to the early days of their marriage.

Jessica risked a glance at Quinn, who was viewing the drama with resignation. When he caught her eye, he surprised her by winking. Realizing this was standard operating procedure for the couple, Jessica allowed her mind to wander as Sylvia began berating Keith for showing up a half hour late to their wedding.

Quinn looked tired, Jessica considered, surreptitiously eyeing his drawn expression. He was sporting a dark tan, obviously a souvenir from his trip to Mexico with Pamela Stuart, but his skin seemed more tightly drawn over his bones. His green eyes were devoid of that sparkling gleam she had often thought of during their time apart, and lines bracketed his lips. Those wonderful, seductive lips...

A sudden knock on the door captured Jessica's attention and a moment later her secretary entered, the heretofore unflappable Paula obviously distressed.

"There's a telephone call for you, Ms O'Neill."

"Please take a message, Paula," Jessica requested.

"It's an emergency," Paula stated. Her voice cracked, causing Jessica's blood to freeze in her veins. "Oh God, Jessica, I'm sorry."

The girls, Jessica thought dazedly as she made her way over to the phone in the corner of the room. Her heart was pounding in her throat and she screamed a silent prayer that they were all right. The image of that little boy this morning swam before her eyes. What if that had been Sara? Oh, dear God, she begged. Please don't let it be that!

Quinn was on his feet, staring helplessly at Jessica as he watched her face go ashen, her eyes close. "I understand," she managed to respond, her voice not much above a whisper. "I'll be right there."

But she remained frozen, her eyes staring at some unseen location out the window. Quinn was by her side in two long strides, taking the telephone receiver from her icy hands.

"Jess?" he asked, his hands cupping her shoulders as he shook her gently, dragging her attention toward him. "What is it? Not the girls?"

She could have wept at the wealth of concern in his eyes, and managed to shake her head. "No," she said on a deep, ragged breath. "Not the girls."

"Thank God!" He exhaled a deep, relieved breath of his own. "Then what?"

Her hands clasped his upper arm, her fingernails digging into the flesh covered by his gray suit. "Oh, Quinn," she said on a weak, broken sob, "it's my home. There was a fire." Tears welled up in her eyes. "Everything's gone, Quinn. Everything."

Knowing how much the house had meant to Jessica, understanding how it had symbolized her hard-won independence, Quinn drew her into his arms, holding her tight, his hands stroking her hair, her back.

"Listen to me," he said gently, putting her a little away. "It's going to be okay. Do you hear me?"

She stared at him uncomprehendingly.

"Listen to me, Jess," he repeated, his voice firmer, his tone more self-assured. "We're going to go there. Together. And I promise everything is going to turn out fine. You've got to believe me, honey."

She leaned into him, resting her forehead against his chest, taking deep breaths as she drew from his strength. When she lifted her head, her eyes glistened with tears.

"I'm so glad you're here, Quinn," she whispered.

He gave her a long, hard kiss on the lips. "Me too, babe," he murmured huskily. "Me too."

Then he led her to the door, turning back toward an avidly interested pair of onlookers.

"You two work something out," he ordered. "We've got more important things to do than watch you idiots fight."

Ignoring their shocked expressions, he left the conference room. "Ms O'Neill won't be in for a few days," he instructed Paula firmly, preparing for an argument from Jessica. Quinn was disturbed when she failed to offer the slightest protest and realized she was obviously in a state of shock. "Would you reschedule her appointments?"

"Of course," Paula answered immediately, reaching for her appointment calendar.

"Oh," Quinn added on an afterthought, "would you please call my office and tell them I won't be back today?"

"I already did."

Quinn managed to reward Paula with a weak smile, wondering why it was that everyone else saw what Jessica appeared blind to. That however loudly she wanted to protest the fact, they belonged together. Permanently.

And he was going to make her see that if it was the last thing he did.

11

THE SIDEWALK WAS CROWDED with onlookers as Quinn pulled up in front of the smoldering ruins of what had once been Jessica's beloved home.

The outer walls of the Victorian house were still standing, but the windowpanes had been blown out by the intense heat. Through the gaping holes, Quinn could view the charred interior.

"What do they all want?" she asked weakly. "Why are they here?"

"I suppose it's curiosity. And a certain sense of relief that it didn't happen to them."

"Oh, Quinn," she half sobbed, "I think I just discovered that I'm a terrible person."

He took both her hands in his, his heart torn at her despairing expression. "Nonsense," he objected firmly. "What on earth gave you that idea?"

Her eyes were bleak as they turned to the crowd of gaping bystanders. "I wish it had been one of them," she whispered harshly. "I wish it had been anyone but me." She shook her head and covered her face with her hands.

Quinn drew her into his arms, stroking her back. "That's only natural, sweetheart," he assured her. "There isn't anything wrong with you." He gazed down into her stricken face. "Let me take you to my place," he suggested. "There isn't anything you can do here."

Jessica shook her head. "No. I want to see everything, Quinn."

"Are you sure? Look, honey, we can call your insurance company from my apartment. It's going to take them a while to start the claims process, anyway. You should be resting."

A thought suddenly occurred to Quinn. "We need to do something about the girls. They shouldn't be coming home to this."

At the idea of her daughters, safe with Brian in Marin County, Jessica experienced a cool wave of relief. It was only a house, she reminded herself. Boards and shingles. It could be replaced. Her children couldn't.

"They're all right," she managed through tight lips. "They didn't have school today. Mallory wanted to show Brian her movie, so they're spending the weekend with him."

"Then her tapes didn't burn?"

At the honest relief in his voice, Jessica was once again reminded of what a very nice man Quinn could be. "No, thank God. She's too young to realize that this isn't the end of the world."

"How about you? Can you realize that?"

Jessica took a deep breath. "I've been through worse," she admitted. "I can probably survive this, as well."

"I've no doubt of that," he agreed, wiping away the moisture on her cheeks with his handkerchief. "But are you sure you want to go in there right now?"

"I have to. I have to see if there's anything left."

Quinn looked over her shoulder, doubting that anything had survived the inferno that had gutted Jessica's home. *God,* he thought, his stomach clenching, *if this had happened last night, with Jessica asleep upstairs . . .* The idea was too unpalatable to consider further.

"Let's get it over with," he suggested grimly, opening the car door.

Jessica held tight to his hand as they walked toward the still smoldering house. As they approached, the crowd parted like the waters of the Red Sea, allowing them to pass. Jessica was numbly aware of Quinn speaking to the firemen who were cleaning up the destruction, but she didn't know what they were saying. Neither did she care.

The front door, with its lovely stained glass window, had been hacked to splinters by the firefighters' axes, Jessica noted dully. She stood in the open doorway, her eyes bleak as she viewed the devastation. It was all gone—Jill's wild clothes, Sara's scrapbook, her paintings. Everything. She moaned.

The soft sound drew Quinn's attention. "Are you sure you're all right?"

"I don't know," Jessica said, swaying slightly as her head began to swim.

Black dots appeared before her eyes and she prayed that she wouldn't disgrace herself by fainting in public. She'd never fainted before in her life. But neither had she had the misfortune to witness her life gone up in flames.

"I'm taking you home," Quinn stated brusquely, his firm tone assuring Jessica that he wasn't listening to any further objections.

"I don't have a home."

Her face was an unhealthy shade of gray, and her eyes appeared wider than usual. The shadows beneath them, which had been so evident only an hour ago were even darker and deeper.

"My home."

"Oh."

Jessica remembered little else after that. She was vaguely aware of Quinn leading her to his car, where she was able to lean her head against the back of the seat, closing her eyes against the swirling vertigo that threatened to overcome her. She offered no objection as he took her directly to his bedroom, sitting her down on the edge of the bed before proceeding to undress her.

He knelt on the lush burnt umber carpeting, slipping her pumps from her feet. His fingers made quick work of the buttons on the front of the blue silk dress, and she shrugged her shoulders, allowing him to push the material down to her waist. He laid her gently on the mattress, pulling the dress down over her hips. Her nylons followed, then her half-slip, until she was clad only in her lacy bra and panties.

When Quinn slid her under the chocolate-brown sheets, Jessica closed her eyes as her head sank into the pillow. She couldn't remember being so tired, so wrung out. Then she felt him moving away and her eyes flew open.

"Where are you going?"

"Just into the other room. I'm calling a doctor."

She shook her head. "I don't need a doctor."

"You're in shock," he said. "When it settles in, you're going to be upset. I want to get you something."

"I don't take tranquilizers," she argued weakly, finding speech a major effort. "They're habit-forming."

"One damn pill isn't going to turn you into an addict, Jess," Quinn shot back. "Dammit, for once in your life would you stop being so stubborn and let someone help you?" His concern for her made his voice gravelly, his words harsh.

"I don't need any pills," she repeated. "I need you, Quinn."

Quinn was aware that Jessica was not herself. She never would have admitted that under normal conditions. And certainly not on such a soft, pleading tone. Shaking his head, he sat down beside her, pushing her hair back from her face with unsteady fingers.

"I worry about you, babe."

Her hand reached out for him, then fell to the sheet, as if the movement required more strength than she possessed.

"I know," she whispered. "Please don't leave me, Quinn." Her blue eyes were eloquent pools of need, pulling him into their swirling depths.

Quinn suddenly felt as if he were drowning. "At least let me call the insurance company for you," he suggested, wanting to spare Jessica that initial piece of bureaucratic red tape.

"All right. I got a renewal notice yesterday," she said flatly. "It's still in my purse. I think the number's on that."

"I'll call them and be right back."

"Quinn?"

He turned in the doorway. "What is it, sweetheart?"

"Please don't be gone long."

He returned to the side of the bed, bending down to brush a light, reassuring kiss against her lips. "Don't worry," he vowed. "I won't leave you alone."

She nodded, closing her eyes, crying silently as she viewed the horrid images emblazoned on her mind. It was only a short time later that Jessica felt Quinn lie down beside her. She didn't have the strength to open her eyes, but her fingers inched across the sheet, unerringly locating his hand.

"You came back."

He linked their fingers together, bringing her hand to his lips. "Of course."

"I'm glad," she murmured drowsily. She was so tired! How could she want so badly to sleep in the middle of the day? "I don't know what I would have done if you hadn't been with me today, Quinn."

"I'll always be there for you, Jess. That's a promise."

"Ummm." Her breathing was deeper, and a soft pink color was returning gradually to her complexion.

Quinn drew her into his arms, fitting her comfortably, safely against him. Then his gaze grew thoughtful as he watched her sleep.

WHEN JESSICA AWOKE several hours later, the sun was just setting, filling the room with an orange glow. Momentarily disoriented, she glanced around her. Then her gaze lifted to collide with Quinn's.

"Oh, my God," she groaned, seeing the concern etched onto his harshly set features. "It wasn't a nightmare, was it?"

"No. I'm so very sorry, Jess."

"The girls," she remembered suddenly, struggling to sit up. "I have to talk to them."

"I already did. They're fine. Worried about you, of course, but I assured them that their mother is a trooper. The insurance investigator also called. It was the wiring," he stated, confirming what Jessica had already guessed.

She put her arms around him, pressing her cheek against his shirt. "I feel so empty, Quinn. I keep thinking that I should be crying my eyes out. Or screaming at the top of my lungs about the injustice of it all. But I can't feel anything."

"That's understandable. You're bound to be a little numb right now," he assured her, his long fingers combing through the strands of her tousled hair. The auburn waves smelled of smoke.

"Want a shower?" he suggested. "You'd probably feel a little better."

Jessica nodded slowly. "That might help," she agreed.

"I'll fix you something to eat."

"I don't think I could keep anything down," she protested softly.

He lowered his head, kissing her lightly on the forehead. "Just some soup and maybe a sandwich. I've got some chicken. How does that sound?"

She lifted her shoulders in a weary shrug. "You don't have to go to any trouble for me, Quinn."

"I like to do things for you," he argued. "You never let me do enough as it is. At least let me feed you." His judicious gaze skimmed her body, which appeared unusually slender under the crisp dark sheet. "Besides, you've lost weight. Obviously you need someone to take care of you."

She sighed, unable to work up the strength to argue further. "All right."

Quinn smiled down at her. Then he went into the adjoining bathroom and soon Jessica could hear the sound of running water.

"Can you make it into the bathroom yourself?" he asked with concern as he returned. "Do you need help washing your hair?"

"I'll be fine." Her voice was unsteady, but her eyes offered Quinn assurance.

"I never had a single doubt about that," he agreed. "I left my robe in the bathroom for you. It'll be too big, but your clothes smell of smoke, and you've got that stain on your dress."

Was it only this morning that her worst problem had been spilled coffee? It seemed like a lifetime ago.

"Thank you, Quinn. You're very nice."

As he left the room to fix Jessica something to eat, Quinn considered that "nice" was not how he wanted her to see him. Teddy bears were nice; television weathermen were nice; Quinn wanted to be Jessica's overwhelming passion. He wanted her to be as obsessed with him as he was with her.

He'd gone crazy while he'd been in Phoenix with Keith. It had taken every ounce of his willpower not to pick up the phone and call Jessica, agreeing to whatever she was willing to offer. The knife blade flashed dangerously as he hacked away at the cold roast chicken with angry strokes.

Quinn's irritation disintegrated when Jessica appeared in the kitchen doorway a while later, offering him a slightly wobbly smile.

"That was a good idea. I feel better."

"You look marvelous," he said, gazing at the lovely woman wrapped in the voluminous folds of his navy robe.

Her hair fell wetly over her shoulders, and her skin, what little of it was visible, shone pinkly, as if she'd attempted to scrub away not only the smoke, but the memory of the fire, as well. She looked soft and vulnerable, and although he knew this was a hell of a time to be having such thoughts, deliciously desirable.

"Hungry?" he asked with studied casualness, turning away so Jessica couldn't view his body's reaction to her pleasantly disheveled state.

"Yes."

Her tone was soft, inviting sensual fantasies, and Quinn wondered what kind of man he was to be experiencing sexual hunger at a time like this. Jessica needed someone to take care of her right now. To comfort her.

"Good. I've made sandwiches and the soup's warming. I hope you like cream of asparagus. It's canned. But it's good."

Jessica stared at his back, wondering what to do next. She'd seen the way his eyes had darkened with unmasked desire when he'd looked at her. She knew that whatever had happened to their affair, the attraction between them was as strong and viable as ever.

"I am hungry, Quinn," she agreed, moving quietly across the room on bare feet and putting her arms around his waist. "But not for food." She pressed her cheek against his back, fitting her body intimately against his.

"Jess," Quinn warned raggedly, "do you have any idea what you're doing?"

"Yes," she answered simply.

He spun around propelling her soft curves against him with harsh, unforgiving strength. "Damn you, Jessie," he groaned, his fingers tangling painfully in the wet strands of her hair. "Damn you for making me need you like this!"

Then his mouth came down hard and demanding on hers, his tongue thrusting deeply with a greedy passion that threatened to devour her. His strong fingers splayed against the back of her head as he held her to the blazing kiss.

Her soft cry against his lips only served to fuel Quinn's spiraling passion. He scooped her up, his lips fused to hers as he carried her back into the bedroom. The soft velour robe was no obstacle as his hands moved over her breasts, his fingers kneading the flesh, creating a pleasure that was just this side of pain. In turn, Jessica's fingers tore at the buttons of his shirt, her palms pressing against the warm, moist skin of his chest.

When she dragged her mouth away from his to trail a series of stinging kisses from the base of his throat to his navel, Quinn thought he'd explode. A groan rumbled in his throat as he felt her soft breath against the wool of his pants and then he was tearing them off, Jessica helping him, her own need every bit as desperate.

Tenderness gave way to hunger, both of them giving and taking pleasure as they drove each other mad with passion. Quinn's hot moist breath burned her skin, creating an ache deep inside her as he relentlessly drove her closer and closer to the very brink of sanity. His lips and hands were everywhere, tasting, touching, creating havoc with her senses.

In turn, Jessica explored the hard lines of his body, thrilled by the way he trembled under her touch. Then his fingers dug into her waist and she gasped as he lowered her onto him, filling her with his rigid strength.

"Oh, Quinn," she cried out, leaning forward, the pebbled tips of her breasts brushing his chest. "I think I'm burning up!"

"That's right," he growled, his fingers clutching her hips, thrusting more deeply into her. "Flame for me, Jess. Let me feel your fire!"

Her body was a torch, alive with a heated passion that threatened to consume her. Jessica could only wonder what it was about Quinn that made her go so wildly, primitively out of control.

His tongue explored the moistness of her mouth, thrusting into all the warm dark corners as his movements became faster, deeper. Jessica's entire body was trembling with ecstasy. Finally, she could contain herself no longer and cried out, calling his name from the very depths of her soul.

Her unrestrained response had a shattering effect on Quinn. His mouth clamped over hers with a harsh moan and his body stiffened as he arched against her. His last coherent thought was that despite her continual assertions to the contrary, Jessica O'Neill was his woman. His and his alone.

Jessica's cheek rested on Quinn's warm chest, her hair spread in damp auburn tangles across his body. Her legs were still wrapped around his and the feel of his strong, hair-roughened thighs against hers was intensely satisfying. His heart had slowed to a more reasonable rhythm, and as her lips pressed against his moist skin, Jessica felt his quick intake of breath.

"You are a wanton," he said, his voice rumbling from deep within his body. "I think you've killed me."

Jessica's cheeks grew pink as she considered her wild, primitive response to Quinn's lovemaking. And she understood why he'd chosen to display such passion, rather than a solicitous tenderness.

He had known exactly what was necessary to take her mind from the fire and her troubles. He'd known precisely what to do. As it seemed he always did. She breathed a sad, rippling little sigh.

"Don't," he requested softly, his fingers playing with her hair. "Don't have any regrets."

She lifted her head, her blue eyes solemn. "I don't," she murmured truthfully. "At least not about what we just did. I love making love to you, Quinn."

She gave him a faint smile. "In fact, I can't think of anything else I'd rather be doing." Her fingers toyed nervously with the dark hair covering his chest. "I think I've become a Quinn Masterson junkie."

"Is that so bad?" he inquired with what he considered amazing calmness. He certainly didn't feel that way inside.

Jessica sighed, rolling over onto her back to stare thoughtfully at the ceiling. Not knowing what he could say to forestall her probable answer, Quinn remained silent.

"When I was younger," she said finally, her gaze still directed upward, "my entire life revolved around my family. I was Elizabeth and Mac's daughter, then I was Brian's wife. We weren't married a year before I was Jill's mother, then Mallory's, then Sara's. I only viewed myself in relation to others."

When Quinn failed to comment, Jessica turned her head on the pillow. "I know you can't possibly understand that. But after Brian left me, I realized I had absolutely no idea who Jessica O'Neill was. Who she really was."

"I think I can empathize with that," he argued.

She shook her head. "No, Quinn, you can't," she insisted quietly. "You can sympathize, but you can't empathize." Her somber blue eyes held a certain fondness. "I've the impression you sprang from the womb knowing who you were, what you wanted to do, where you were going in life."

He sat up now, the muscles in his jaw firming as he looked down at her. "You're wrong there," he pointed out brusquely. "Do you know how many times I still feel like I'm playing a role? That I'm still just some dirt poor Missouri farm kid?"

His green eyes turned hard. "Hell, yes, I can empathize with you, but I don't want to play word games, Jess! Sympathize, empathize, what difference does it make? I love you, damn it! That's all that matters."

"If it were only that simple," she said softly, gazing bleakly up at the ceiling once more.

"Do you love me?" he asked suddenly.

"Why do you insist on asking that?" she whispered. "It wouldn't really matter."

Quinn hit the sheet with his fist. "It would to me. I need to know, Jessica. Do you love me or not?"

When she slowly, regretfully turned her glistening eyes back to his, Jessica's face was a portrait of despair. She wept silently, unaware of the tears streaming down her cheeks.

"Oh, Quinn," she said on a sigh that was part moan, turning her head toward the wall, unable to view the need swirling in his stormy green eyes.

What did the man want, Jessica asked herself desperately. She'd given him her body; she'd shared her most intimate feelings, told him of doubts and fears that she'd never revealed to another living soul. She'd even let him into her daughters' lives, something she had always sworn never to do with any man she might date.

But still he wanted more. In that respect, she considered ruefully, Quinn was no different from any other man. He wanted too much. Because he wanted everything. He wanted more than she could possibly ever give.

His fingers cupped her downcast chin and turned her head back toward him. When she would have turned away again, he wouldn't permit it.

"I asked you a question, Jess," he reminded her softly. "And I'm still waiting for an answer."

"Why are you doing this?" she shouted, swiping at her tears. "Haven't I had enough grief today without you making things worse?" The last was flung at him on a wail, and

Quinn closed his eyes, unable to view the misery etching ugly lines on her face.

Jessica had to press her hands together to keep from reaching up to stroke the rigid line of his jaw. If this was what love did, she thought miserably, if it could destroy two people like this, then she wished she'd never experienced its treachery.

But then, she considered honestly, she'd have never known the heights of passion and the sheer joy found in being with the man she loved. Why couldn't it have stayed that way, she agonized. Why did he have to ruin everything?

She watched Quinn's chest rise and fall as he sighed soundlessly. Then he opened his eyes and she was shocked at the raw pain she saw there.

"Oh, Jess," he groaned. "I never wanted to hurt you like this. I never wanted to hurt *us* like this."

Quinn knew Jessica was aching as badly as he was at the moment and wanted nothing more than to pull her into his arms, to bury his head between her soft breasts and drink in her sweet scent. He wanted her soothing hands to stroke his flesh, to quiet this pain.

He wanted to make love to her forever; he wanted to immerse himself in her flesh, in her love. He wanted to beg her to stay, to assure her that whatever their problems, they could work them out. But Quinn knew that although Jessica was willing to turn to him in moments of desperation and need, she wasn't ready to make a lasting commitment.

She wanted to be strong, he thought angrily. The ironic thing was that he'd never met a woman capable of turning him inside out like this. He wondered what it would take to make Jessica realize that she was far more self-sufficient than she secretly believed. Enough so that marrying him wouldn't cost her her hard-earned independence.

"The soup will have evaporated down to nothing," he said flatly, his feet hitting the floor as he turned away from her.

Jessica longed to run her hands across the hard lines of his shoulders, but resisted, knowing that it would be unfair to give Quinn contradictory messages.

"I'm not that hungry," she protested softly. "If you'll just call a cab, I'll go to a hotel."

Quinn ground his teeth, suddenly understanding those crimes of passion that were always cropping up on the six o'clock news. He rose from the bed and glared down at her.

"Don't be an idiot, you don't even have any clothes. You're staying here tonight. Tomorrow we'll have Elizabeth bring over some clothes, then we'll—excuse me—*you*," he corrected harshly, "can decide what you're going to do."

"That makes sense," she murmured in a subdued voice. "Thank you, Quinn. This is very kind of you."

He slammed his fist into his palm. One of these days, Quinn decided, after he and Jessica were married, he was going to have a long talk with Mac and find out how the man managed to live all those years with Jessica's mother. Because from what he'd been able to tell, Jessica didn't fall far from the genetic tree when it came to an extra helping of pigheaded stubbornness.

"I'm not doing this out of kindness," he roared, losing patience entirely. "And if I were you, Jess, I'd shut up before you find out exactly how low I am on that particular commodity right now.

"In fact, I'm about ready to double bolt that door and keep you in that bed while I make love to you until you can't move. That might be as effective a method of keeping you here where you belong as any others I might try!"

Jessica was not immune to the anger blazing in his eyes, but neither could she remain unaffected by the sudden flare of desire she viewed there, either. She chewed nervously at her bottom lip, inciting a muffled groan from Quinn. His fingers, as they thrust through his hair, were far from steady.

There was so much he wanted to say. So many things he needed to tell her. Beginning with how much he loved her. And ending with the fact that he always would.

"I'd better check on your dinner," he said instead. Then he left the room.

12

IF JESSICA HAD TO PICK one word to describe the mood the next morning, it would have been "cautious." Both she and Quinn seemed to be walking on eggs, neither anxious to renew the argument that had threatened to blaze out of control last night.

She'd called Elizabeth, who agreed to bring her something to wear; fortunately, her mother had kept her youthful figure and both women wore the same size. Then Jessica had called her daughters, relieved to find that they were amazingly unconcerned about the fire. Staying in Marin County for a few more days gave them a holiday from school, and a chance to swim in their father's new pool.

"I have to admit that surprises me," Jessica said, as she shared a Spartan breakfast of cold cereal and coffee with Quinn. She hadn't wanted to eat even that, but Quinn had insisted, and she didn't have the strength to argue this morning. "I expected them to be in tears."

"Kids are pretty resilient," he replied, slicing a banana atop the cornflakes.

"Fortunately," she agreed.

"How are you feeling?"

She shrugged. "Like I've been run over by a Mack truck," she admitted.

His gaze fell to her arm, which bore a lingering bruise from last night's lovemaking.

"I'm sorry."

Her eyes held a spark of humor, the first he'd seen since the day he'd stormed out of her house. "I'm not. I wasn't referring to that, Quinn."

"Oh."

They both fell quiet again and an uncomfortable silence settled over the room.

"Want a section of the morning paper?" Quinn asked politely.

Following his cue, Jessica nodded. "Thank you."

"Which part? Fashion? You can check out the sales."

"Business, I think," she decided. "The idea of all that clothes shopping is too depressing.... Unless you want the business section," she tacked on with consummate politeness.

"No, it's yours," he offered, handing her the pages, hating this conversation that could have been taking place between two strangers.

"Thank you," she repeated.

"You're welcome."

Jessica hoped Elizabeth would hurry. She couldn't take much more of Quinn's studiously proper manners. She eyed her coffee cup, wondering what he'd do if she suddenly dumped the cooling contents into his lap.

Quinn caught Jessica's thoughtful study of her cup. "Would you like some more coffee?"

"No, thank you."

"Would you like it warmed up?"

She smiled a stiff little smile. "Thanks, but it's fine."

"You're sure?"

"Positive."

"All right. If you want anything, just ask."

"Do you mean that?" she said suddenly.

Quinn's spoon stopped on the way to his mouth and he slowly lowered it back to the bowl. "Of course. What can I get for you? Some toast? An omelet?"

Jessica shook her head firmly. "I don't want anything else to eat."

He arched an inquiring brow. "Then what?"

"Could you stop treating me like I'm visiting royalty? I'm starting to get very nervous, Quinn."

His level gaze met hers. "I was only trying to keep things on an even keel."

"Do you think that's honestly possible?" Jessica asked shakily.

There was a lengthy silence from across the table. "Between us?" he finally inquired.

Jessica knew it to be a rhetorical question and didn't bother to answer. As she watched warily, his eyes seemed to harden and something flickered in their depths. She flinched as he reached across the table, his fingers braceleting her wrist.

"Between us?" he repeated, turning her hand over, tracing thoughtful little circles on her palm with his index finger.

There was nothing overtly sexual in the gesture, but Jessica felt a heat building deep within her feminine core, sending little eddies of flaming current spiraling outward to warm her entire body.

Quinn's emerald eyes gleamed with beguiling satisfaction as he felt the pulse rate under his fingers increase. Jessica unconsciously licked her lips, and as he watched, her expression softened and a soft pink hue darkened her cheeks. When she dragged her gaze away from his stroking finger to meet his, her eyes were melted sapphires, dark, lustrous, shining with shared desire.

"No, Jess," he assured her in a rough voice. "Nothing between us could ever remain on an even keel. When we fight, I suppose we'll fight tooth and nail," he grated. "But when we love, Jessie—ah, there's nothing that equals the storm we make. You can't deny that, sweetheart."

Jessica tugged, retrieving her hand, lowering it to her lap where Quinn couldn't view her fingers twisting nervously together.

"No," she admitted softly. "I've never felt the way I do when I make love with you, Quinn. It's indescribable. But we can't spend the rest of our lives in bed."

"I don't know," he drawled. "The idea is rather intriguing, now that you mention it. Although we'd probably have to plan ahead and stock the freezer." His eyes gleamed with a wicked light, enticing her to give up the battle. "I wouldn't want you wasting away to nothing."

"Dammit, Quinn," Jessica snapped. "This isn't a time for you to pull out your well-honed seduction techniques!"

"Correct me if I'm mistaken," he said with a silkiness that didn't mask the gravelly note in his voice, "but you were the one doing most of the seducing last night." He allowed a wry smile. "Not that I'm complaining, you understand. I just want to get that little fact down on the record."

He was right, Jessica admitted secretly. But even then it had been an act of surrender. She'd given in to the primitive hunger he was able to instill in her with a single word, a single glance or touch. Whenever she was with Quinn, tides of emotion lapped away at her willpower, dissolving it like a sandcastle at high tide.

Quinn hated the way her face suddenly closed, denying him access to her thoughts. "Jessica?"

When she slowly, reluctantly lifted her gaze to his, her eyes were filled with self-loathing that tore at some delicate fiber deep inside him.

"I was just thinking of a line from T. S. Eliot," she murmured. "And how it seemed to fit me lately."

"Are you going to let me in on it?" he asked quietly.

Jessica braced her elbows on the table, rubbing wearily at her temples. "He wrote of the awful daring that's involved in a moment's surrender," she said tightly.

Quinn swore softly. "Why in hell do you insist on putting up these artificial barriers between us?"

"Because they're real," she retorted harshly. "What we have in there—" she tossed her head in the direction of the bedroom "—is one thing. But it isn't enough to base a lifetime relationship on."

"What do you know about lifetime relationships?" he blazed. "You went into this with the intention of having a nice, brief little affair. No strings. No commitment on either side!"

With a swift movement Jessica had been totally unprepared for, Quinn was suddenly standing over her, closing his hands over her shoulders, hauling her unceremoniously to her feet.

"You're a fine one to talk, sweetheart. All you ever wanted from me was sex. I'd say if anyone should be feeling used right about now, it's me." His green gaze raked her scornfully. "Admit it—you used me for stud service. Sexual relief for the frustrated divorcée, right?"

The sound rang out like a gunshot and Jessica stared at the hand still resting on his cheek.

"Feel better?" he drawled dangerously.

Jessica's eyes remained riveted on the red mark disfiguring his harsh features as she slowly lowered her hand to her side. Then she shrugged free, turning away. "I hate what you do to me," she whispered. "I hate the way you make me lose control."

Quinn studied the slump to her slender shoulders, telling himself that he'd gone about that all wrong. He hadn't meant to get into an argument with her. He damn well hadn't intended to say those things. He and Jessica were like a flammable vapor meeting fire; the explosion was inevitable.

"Jess—" he tried what he hoped was a consoling tone "—I'm sorry. You made me angry and I said some things I didn't mean."

Her response was muffled, but he wasn't encouraged as she shook her head, refusing to turn around.

He moved to her, putting his arms around her. Jessica tensed at the intimate touch. "Honey, you frustrated me. You keep confusing what you feel is surrender in bed, to surrender in life."

"Isn't it?" she whispered.

He rested his chin on her auburn hair. "If it is, then we're both in the same boat because I can't keep away from you any more than you can keep away from me."

"You did a damn good job of it the past three weeks," she complained. "How was Mexico, by the way?"

"Mexico?" he asked, sounding confused. "What gave you the idea I was in Mexico?"

Perhaps he hadn't been with Pamela Stuart, after all. Although Jessica experienced a fleeting sense of relief, she reminded herself that it changed nothing. She merely shrugged.

"I was in Phoenix with Keith."

"You didn't return my calls."

"I wanted to. I must have picked up the phone a hundred times a day, but I was afraid you wouldn't want to hear anything I had to say. . . .

"I was going crazy from missing you, Jess." Quinn's voice held a rough, masculine plea. "Doesn't that mean anything?"

"Only that we're just like the Thackers. We can't live with each other, and we can't live without each other." She turned, lifting her distressed gaze to his. "Well, I don't know about you, but I can't go on this way. I'm not going to see you again, Quinn."

A flicker of pain flashed in his eyes, but his voice was steady. His appraising gaze surveyed her tense face.

"This conversation is all too familiar," he grated. "Be certain this is what you really want this time, Jessica," he warned softly. "Because I'm not going to keep setting myself up to be dumped like this."

Jessica stared at Quinn as his words slowly sank in. Is that what she'd done to him? Was she no better than Brian? Had she just taken what he had to offer, then turned her back and walked away, rather than offering a commitment? Oh God, she groaned inwardly, how had things gotten so confused?

Quinn watched the waves of emotion washing over Jessica's face. First confusion, then doubt, then a blinding comprehension so powerful that it caused her to tremble in his arms. He released her, allowing her to slump wearily into her chair as he waited for her to retract her incautious words.

The sound of the doorbell fractured the thick silence. Quinn's oath was brief and harsh. Refusing to leave this matter unsettled, he remained standing over Jessica, his mouth a hard, grim line. The doorbell rang again. Then, when he continued to ignore it, one more time.

"You'd better answer your door," Jessica suggested on a flat, defeated note. "I don't think whoever is out there is going to go away." The strident demand of the bell proved her correct.

He looked over his shoulder to the foyer with a withering glance. Then his gaze returned to Jessica. "This is more important."

When the chimes pealed again, Jessica exhaled a deep sigh. "We're not going to be able to discuss anything with all that racket," she pointed out. "Go open the door, Quinn."

Muttering a particularly violent series of expletives, Quinn marched to the door, flinging it open with ill-concealed anger. He had to swallow his planned response as he viewed Elizabeth, standing in the hallway, a red suitcase in her hand.

"I was beginning to think you weren't home," she said, her smile wavering as she viewed Quinn's harshly set features. "Perhaps I'd better just give you this and leave," Elizabeth suggested, shoving the overnight case at him.

Jessica experienced a mixture of regret and relief when she heard her mother's voice. "Mom?" she called out, getting up from the chair. "You don't have to go."

"Quinn?" Elizabeth asked sympathetically.

He shrugged with feigned carelessness, taking the suitcase from her hand. "What the hell," he muttered, "we're not getting anywhere, anyway. You might as well come in."

Elizabeth embraced her daughter, her judicial gaze deciding that as bad as Jessica looked, Quinn appeared even worse, if that were possible.

"I brought your clothes," she explained needlessly. "How are you feeling?"

"I've felt better," Jessica admitted.

Elizabeth glanced around the apartment. "I talked with Brian this morning. He has to go out of town for a couple of weeks, but Deirdre said the girls could stay with her."

"No way," Jessica said firmly, crossing her arms over her chest.

Elizabeth nodded understandingly. "I told him that you'd probably want to pick them up this afternoon," she agreed. "Since it doesn't look as if Quinn has room for them here, why don't you let them stay with your father and me?"

Jessica could feel Quinn's hard green eyes impaling her as if they were shafts of cold steel. She had never seen him as angry as he had been this morning. She forced her attention back to her mother.

"Thanks, but they have to finish up these last weeks of school and you and Dad live across town. The insurance will pay for us to move into a hotel while the house is being rebuilt."

Her mother's expression remained smooth, but her voice demonstrated confusion. "But I thought you were staying here."

"I was only a convenient port in the storm," Quinn offered sarcastically. "Jessica never had any intention of staying with me." His tone made it clear that he was talking about more than living arrangements.

Elizabeth's gaze moved first from Jessica, then to Quinn, then back to her daughter. "I see," she said quietly. "Well, dear, why don't you change and I'll drive you up to Mill Valley."

"Thank you," Jessica said, eager to escape Quinn's gaze as she took the suitcase he handed her. There was a spark and an instant of heat when their fingers touched, but his eyes displayed no emotion. As Jessica left the room, she felt unreasonably like a crab scuttling away in the sand.

Ten minutes later she was standing in the doorway, trying to come up with appropriate words to say goodbye. Quinn's expression was unreadable, but she thought she could see a weary depression in his eyes. Jessica's throat tightened.

"Uh, thank you," she said softly. "For everything."

"You're welcome," he answered politely. Then an acid tone slid into his voice. "For everything."

Jessica and Quinn studied each other, each waiting the other out. Then, unable to stand the pain another moment, Jessica spun on her heel, leaving the apartment.

Elizabeth remained quiet on the drive north to Marin County, a fact for which Jessica was exceedingly grateful. She stared out at the rugged coastline, unable to forget Quinn standing there in the foyer, his hands thrust deeply into his front pockets, a raw expression of pain on his face. Jessica knew that image would remain with her for the rest of her life.

13

THE GIRLS FOUND life in a hotel an absolute lark for the first five days. Then they began to complain incessantly about the lack of privacy, the tiny portable refrigerator and the fact that their music had to be kept to a reasonable volume. Jessica was grateful that school would be out in another week. Then, since her parents were taking off to sail the high seas, she might take them up on their offer to use their home.

One advantage to living in a hotel, Jessica decided, was room service. Of course, anything would be an improvement over the meals Elizabeth had prepared during her stay in the house. She was sipping on her morning coffee when Jill approached, a tentative expression on her face.

"Mom?"

Jessica looked up and smiled. The punk look had disappeared; in its place was a lovely young girl with glossy hair and a full-skirted cotton sundress.

"Yes, dear?"

"You haven't forgotten next Wednesday, have you?"

"Forget my daughter's junior high school graduation? Don't be silly. Of course I haven't forgotten."

"Gran and Gramps are coming, too." Jill offered.

"I know," Jessica murmured. She had the distinct feeling that something was being left unsaid.

"I want to invite Quinn," Jill blurted out, confirming Jessica's suspicions.

Jessica slowly lowered her cup to its gilt rimmed saucer. "I don't think that would be a very good idea, sweetheart."

Jill's cheeks flamed scarlet. "Well, I don't think it's fair. Just because you were stupid enough to break up with him, I don't think that's any reason for us to suffer."

"Jill, my relationship with Quinn is really none of your business," Jessica stated firmly, rising from the table.

"It is, too!"

Jessica stared at her daughter. Before she could answer, Mallory entered the living room of the two-bedroom suite and offered her opinion.

"Jill's right," she argued. "Even if you don't love Quinn, we do. And we're definitely getting the short end of the stick. He hasn't been to see us for ages."

Jessica's back stiffened at the accusation in her daughter's tone. She slanted a glance at Sara, who was standing in the doorway, watching quietly.

"What's the matter?" Jessica asked dryly. "Don't you have anything to say about all this?"

Her youngest daughter's voice was soft, but firm. "We miss him, Mom."

"We miss him a lot," Mallory seconded.

"A whole bunch," Jill confirmed. "I really want him to come to my graduation, Mom. Please?"

"What makes you think he'll come?"

"He will if you ask him," Jill said, her expression brightening as she took Jessica's question to be a surrender.

"What makes you think I have any influence over him?" Jessica inquired baldly.

"He loves you," Sara said.

"And I suppose you're an expert?" Jessica couldn't resist asking. She was finding this conversation far more painful than she ever could have imagined.

"He asked you to marry him," Jill reminded her.

"That was several weeks ago," Jessica countered. She began gathering up the scattered breakfast dishes and putting them on the serving cart.

"So?" Mallory wasn't going to let her get away that easily.

Jessica managed a careless shrug. "So things change. People change."

"Like you and Dad changed?" Sara asked, her smooth young forehead drawn together into deep, thoughtful frown lines.

Jessica couldn't lie. She'd always tried to be honest with her daughters and she wasn't about to jeopardize their relationship now.

"No, it's different with Quinn," she admitted. "I still care for him very deeply, but..." Jessica drew in a breath. "Things are complicated," she said slowly. "Quinn and I want different things from life."

She managed a weak smile. "That's enough depressing conversation for one morning," she stated firmly. "Now, if you don't hurry, you'll miss your bus and be late for school."

"We're going," Jill said on a resigned note.

Jessica was not that surprised when Sara turned in the doorway. "Mom?" she whispered, her blue eyes grave.

"Yes?"

"Do you love Quinn?"

"Yes, I do," Jessica answered without hesitation.

Puzzlement shadowed her daughter's clear blue eyes. "Then why don't you just tell him that? I'll bet he still wants to marry you."

Jessica shook her head. "It's not that simple, sweetheart," she replied quietly. "Marriage is more complicated than two people simply loving each other."

They all turned and left the suite, but Jessica couldn't miss Mallory's heartfelt words as they made their way to the elevator.

"Boy, if that's what it's like to be an adult, I'm not ever going to grow up!"

"Don't be a dope," Jill argued. "You can't stay a kid forever."

"Peter Pan did," Sara interjected.

"Peter Pan is just a dumb story," Jill scoffed. "Boy, you two are as dopey as Mom."

While that description wasn't the least bit flattering, Jessica experienced an odd sense of relief at the fact that the girls were bickering. That, at least, was normal behavior.

They made it sound so simple, Jessica mused, as she gathered up her purse and briefcase. Two people fall in love, get married and live happily ever after. How nice it would be if that was the way it really was. However, she was living, breathing proof that not all marriages were made in heaven. Then there was always Keith and Sylvia Thacker.

Jessica had not been surprised when the Thackers reconciled, although she wondered how long they'd manage to stay together this time. She was, however, nonplussed when her former client claimed she'd been the very best attorney she'd ever hired, and promised to call her the next time the couple split.

It was at that point Jessica decided that if she needed an additional excuse to quit her job, avoiding the Thackers was probably reason enough. She had accepted the offer from the District Attorney and was honestly amazed when George Bennington not only asked her to stay with the firm, but offered a generous raise as an incentive.

While Jessica was flattered by the knowledge that despite his demanding attitude, George Bennington found her a bright, capable attorney, she remained firm in her decision. She was looking for new frontiers in her work and the District Attorney's office was nothing if not challenging.

For the first time in ages, Jessica found herself looking forward to her future as she prepared to leave for the office. Today she'd clean out her desk, take a month off, then start her life anew. If she was lucky, she might even begin to get over Quinn Masterson, she told herself, brimming over with self-confidence this final Friday at Bennington, Marston, White and Lowell.

A newspaper was lying on her desk as she walked into her office, already open to the society page. As she sat down, Jessica's gaze was arrested by a strikingly familiar face.

"Socialite snares longtime matrimonial holdout," the headline on the gossip column screamed out at her. As Jessica stared at Pamela Stuart's elegant features, an icy fear skimmed its way up her spine. The accompanying story confirmed her worst fears. Pamela had not only announced her engagement to Quinn, they'd set the date for a week from today.

"He's making an enormous mistake," Jessica said aloud. "She's not right for him. She'll only end up hurting him."

And what do you think you did? a little voice inquired from the depths of her mind.

"I did what I had to do for both of us."

You were afraid, the little voice pressed. *You only thought about yourself.*

"I'm entitled," Jessica argued. "After all, look what happened when I spent my life thinking about everyone else *but* me."

Can you honestly compare Quinn with Brian?

"That's not the point," Jessica said heatedly, embarrassed as Vanessa suddenly appeared in the office doorway.

"Jessica?" she asked hesitantly. "Are you alone? I thought I heard you talking to someone."

"Just myself," Jessica explained with feigned cheeriness. "Which means, I suppose, that I'm getting out of here just in time. Don't they say that's the first sign of insanity?"

"Speaking of getting out, I just dropped by to wish you good luck in your new career. It should prove quite a change."

"That's what I'm hoping," Jessica agreed.

The woman's eyes moved to the paper. "I see you've read the news."

Jessica suddenly realized exactly how the newspaper had arrived on her desk. "About Pamela and Quinn?" she asked casually.

"I tried to warn you, Jessica. But you refused to listen."

Vanessa's conciliatory tone couldn't conceal the oddly victorious note, and Jessica wondered why she'd ever thought this woman was her friend. From the beginning, Vanessa had done nothing but offer damning little innuendos concerning Quinn. Professionally, personally, she'd continued to warn Jessica the man was poison.

She looked at Vanessa curiously. "How long have you worked here?"

"Ages. Sometimes it seems like forever. On a good day it only seems like half my life."

Half her life. Vanessa was slightly older than Jessica. And as far as she knew, the woman had never worked for any other firm. All of a sudden, the pieces began to fall into place.

"Did you and Quinn work together?"

Something flickered in the depths of the woman's eyes for a brief instant, so fleeting that if Jessica hadn't been watching carefully, it would have escaped her attention.

"Now that you mention it," Vanessa stated, brushing at some nonexistent wrinkles on her silk suit, "I believe we might have."

It still hurts, Jessica considered, hearing the bitter edge in the woman's voice. She's been carrying around all that pain for years and years, refusing to allow herself a genuine relationship with a man. Jessica couldn't help comparing Vanessa's behavior with her own and found them uncomfortably similar.

"Quinn once told me that he had planned his life very carefully," Jessica ventured.

"He was going to be a partner by age forty," Vanessa agreed bitterly. "Then and only then was he going to get married."

"Knowing Quinn, I imagine he was up front about his plans."

The woman's eyes hardened. "Oh, I'll give him credit for that," she agreed. "But we all hope that we're the one who can change a man's mind, don't we? That he'll love us more than anything else." Her laugh was short and bitter. "Quinn Masterson's first priority has always been himself."

She tossed her head toward the damning newspaper. "As you'll see, he stuck to his master plan."

He certainly had done that, Jessica thought. But he was wrong. So very wrong.

"If you don't mind, Vanessa, I've got a lot of packing to do."

Vanessa shrugged her silk-clad shoulders. "Sure. Good luck in the D.A.'s office—you're going to need it."

Her words were a distant buzz in Jessica's ear, but she managed to slowly decode them. "Thanks," she answered absently. She stared thoughtfully out the window as she considered Quinn's forthcoming marriage.

"Keep in touch," Vanessa stated with a cheery little wave as she left the office.

"I'll do that," Jessica replied automatically, knowing that if she never saw Vanessa again it would be too soon. She finished cleaning out her desk, anxious to leave.

When she returned to the hotel, Jessica tried to put Quinn from her mind, but found it to be an impossible task. The girls were spending the night with Elizabeth and Mac, leaving Jessica alone with her memories.

She went into one of the bedrooms, locating Mallory's award-winning videotape. It took a while to figure out how to hook up the portable VCR to the hotel television, but soon Jessica was sitting in the darkened room, watching selected scenes from her life flickering on the screen in front of her.

In spite of parental prompting, Mallory had not edited out the scene in which Jessica had fallen over Elizabeth's luggage in an attempt to answer the telephone. Little had she known how that single phone call from Sylvia Thacker would change her life.

Despite Mallory's goal of creating a film of the family, Quinn appeared with heartbreaking frequency. And why not, Jessica asked herself, experiencing a jolt of pain as she watched Quinn fasten the silver locket around her neck. In their short time together, he had infiltrated the household of women with amazing ease. There had been times, Jessica recalled, when his presence had seemed more natural than Brian's ever had.

Her heart stopped as she viewed the scene in the kitchen the morning Quinn had casually dropped the bombshell about their marriage. Now, eyeing him more closely, Jessica noted that although his expression was bland enough, his fingers were curved tightly around the handle of his coffee cup, his knuckles white with tension.

As she viewed her own expression, Jessica was stunned to see not the aggravation she had thought she was feeling that morning, but pure, unadulterated fear.

Was she afraid of marriage? Of commitment? Was her demand for total autonomy simply a mask for lingering feelings of insecurity? Had she sent Quinn away because she doubted her ability to hold him? If so, she had done him an injustice. Quinn Masterson would be incapable of cheating on his wife, just as Brian O'Neill was incapable of fidelity.

The screen went blank, but Jessica didn't notice. She rose, pacing the floor as she considered her behavior over the past few months. She had been worried about Quinn's gaining the upper hand in their relationship. But the truth was, she realized belatedly, she had always been the one in control. She had insisted on setting limits, on establishing boundaries, creating obstacles to any deep involvement.

Yet somehow love had blossomed despite her machinations. Somehow she had fallen in love with Quinn, and amazingly enough, he had fallen in love with her. But what had she done to return that love? Nothing. Oh, she'd been more than willing to make love with him, Jessica admitted grimly. But on her terms. And when Quinn finally objected, when he insisted on more—on marriage—she'd sent him away.

In spite of that, the minute she had needed him, Quinn had been there for her. Opening his apartment and his heart, demanding nothing in return. And what had she done in return? Slammed the door in his face again.

"Oh, God," Jessica groaned. "Jill was right. I acted like an absolute dope."

Everything Quinn had done proved that he was not a man to force his will on anyone. Least of all someone he loved. A marriage to him would be one of equals. Two people sharing a life based on common respect. And love. It was, Jessica realized, what she wanted more than anything else in the world. But now, thanks to her blindness, she might have lost her chance.

One thing was clear. Quinn wasn't going to set himself up to be hurt again. If she wanted to resolve things between them, she would have to make the first move.

Picking up the telephone, she dialed Quinn's apartment. She was forced to wait, her nerves screaming as she allowed the number to ring ten times. Then ten more. Finally, an additional ten. When there was still no answer, she slowly replaced the receiver to its cradle.

Jessica paced the floor long into the night, redialing Quinn's number at regular intervals. At two o'clock in the morning she was forced to admit he wasn't coming home. Where was he? With Pamela? Was he at this very moment lying in her arms on satin sheets in some luxuriously decorated penthouse bedroom? That thought was too abominable to even consider.

"It's just as well," Jessica decided aloud as she fell into her own lonely bed. "It'll be better in person, anyway. Telephones are so horribly impersonal."

Refusing to give up hope, she finally fell asleep.

JESSICA AWOKE EARLY the following morning, her resolve intact. After ordering coffee from room service, she called the MacLaughlin home.

Elizabeth answered the phone in a muffled, sleepy voice. "H'llo?"

"Mother," Jessica said, "I need your help."

Elizabeth was instantly awake. "Of course, dear. What can I do for you?"

"Would you mind keeping the girls another night?"

"You know your father and I love having them visit," Elizabeth replied without hesitation. Her voice took on a tone of motherly concern. "You're not ill, are you?"

"No," Jessica answered. "I'm fine. I just have something important to do and if everything works out all right, I won't be home this evening."

"You're going to Quinn."

Jessica was not surprised by Elizabeth's insight. After all, she'd undoubtedly seen that gossip item, as well.

"Yes."

A cheer rang in Jessica's ear. "All right, Mom!" Jill shouted. "It's about time!"

"Jill," Elizabeth scolded, her stern tone giving way to a low chuckle, "it's impolite to listen in on the extension."

"Sorry, Gran. But I just won five dollars in the pool."

"Pool? What pool?" Jessica asked.

"I said you'd get back with Quinn today. Sara bet last night, and Mallory had the weird idea you were going to crash his wedding, like Dustin Hoffman did to Katherine Ross in *The Graduate*."

Despite the fact that her daughter had displayed atrocious manners by eavesdropping on a private conversation, not to mention that all three girls had actually been betting on her love life, Jessica laughed.

"Tell Sara that she would have won if Quinn had been home last night," Jessica revealed.

"Jessie?" Mac's voice came on the line.

"Yes, Dad?"

"Don't worry about a thing. If Quinn doesn't take you back, we'll sue for breach of promise."

"You wouldn't!"

Her father's laugh was rich and deep. "Take your pick, daughter. It's either that or showing up at his office with my shotgun."

"You've never even owned a gun," Jessica protested.

"You know that and I know that. But Quinn Masterson doesn't. I have every intention of seeing my daughter safely married off before I go sailing into the sunset." Mac paused, as if carefully choosing his words.

"What the hell," he continued gruffly. "You may scream bloody murder, but I have to admit I'll feel a lot better knowing that you've got a good man taking care of you while I'm away."

Jessica had no intention of screaming. Because she knew that Quinn would take care of her. Just as she had every intention of taking care of him.

"I love you, Dad," she said softly before hanging up.

Jessica showered and dressed in record time. While she had no idea how Quinn would react to her interference in his life, she refused to allow her determination to falter. As she took a taxi to his office, she hoped it wasn't too late to change things.

The young woman at the desk outside Quinn's office rose as Jessica marched by. "Excuse me, ma'am, but you can't go in without an appointment!"

"D.A.'s office," Jessica announced blithely, ignoring the secretary's protest. "Official business."

Quinn's back was to the door, his gaze directed out the window as he dictated a letter to an elderly stenographer.

"In closing, I believe that Lamberson Electronics can only benefit by the proposed merger and recommend moving to file as quickly as possible. If you have any questions or comments, please don't hesitate to contact me. Sincerely yours, et cetera, et cetera. Could you please read that back to me, Mrs. Young?"

The woman was staring up at Jessica, who'd suddenly appeared beside her, and didn't answer.

"Mrs. Young?" Quinn repeated, turning around in his chair.

When he saw Jessica, an inscrutable mask settled over his features. "Thank you, Mrs. Young," he said, his eyes not leaving Jessica's. "That will be all for today. And please tell Susan to hold all my calls."

"Yes, sir." The woman rose quickly, departing from the room.

Quinn braced his elbows on the arms of his chair, making a tent with his fingers.

"Well, well," he said smoothly. "It's not often I have a visitor from the D.A.'s office. Don't tell me that there's a bench warrant out for my overdue parking tickets?"

He wasn't going to make it easy on her, Jessica thought. Then she gave a mental shrug. Why should he? Since he'd yet to offer her a chair, Jessica remained standing.

"I'm surprised you know about my move," she admitted, wondering when Quinn could have had time to keep tabs on her while courting Pamela Stuart.

"Mac told me. Congratulations, by the way."

"You've been talking to my father?"

Quinn gestured at a chair on the other side of the desk. "Sit down, Jess," he suggested patiently. "And to answer your question, Mac and I were friends long before you and I had our little affair. I'm not going to stop seeing the man just because his daughter walked out on me."

That stung. Jessica looked down at her hands, pretending a sudden interest in her fingernails.

"Jessica?"

She lifted her gaze, looking for something, anything in his smooth green eyes. Some sign that he still cared. Jessica could find nothing there, but she hadn't come here to turn tail and run at the first obstacle.

"Yes?" she asked, managing to match his casual tone.

"You still haven't told me what you're doing here," he reminded her.

Jessica gazed out at the sparkling waters of the bay. The orange expanse of Golden Gate Bridge gleamed copper in the bright sunlight of early June.

She decided to ease into it. "I called you last night, but you weren't home."

"I had a meeting in Sacramento that ran late," he answered easily. "I spent the night there."

"Oh."

The silence settled down between them again. Jessica took a deep breath. It was now or never.

"I've come to save you," she blurted out.

He arched a brow. "Save me?"

She nodded and her tone was a little firmer as she elaborated. "From making the biggest mistake of your life."

"I see." He swiveled back and forth in the chair, eyeing her impassively. "I don't suppose you'd care to explain that a little further," he prompted.

"You can't marry Pamela Stuart," she insisted, leaning forward in her own chair, her body a stiff, tense line. "I know you had this big master plan for your life. But you can't get married just because you've turned forty, Quinn! That's not a good enough reason."

"What *is* a good reason to get married, Jess?" he asked softly.

"Love," she answered without hesitation.

He picked up a gold fountain pen, toying with it absently. Every one of Jessica's nerve endings were screaming with impatience, waiting for Quinn to say something.

"What makes you think I don't love Pam?"

"Because you love me," she stated firmly, her blue eyes daring him to deny that statement.

"You know, Jess, a torch is a damned burdensome thing to carry around forever," he advised her evenly. "After a while it burns down and you end up scorching your fingers."

"And I love you."

Quinn's expression didn't waver. Jessica thought she saw something flash in his eyes, but it was gone too quickly for her to be certain.

"I see . . . When did you come to that momentous conclusion?"

"I think I fell in love with you that first night we met," Jessica admitted softly. "But I knew for certain when we made love the first time."

While Jessica had not known what reaction she was going to receive by coming here today, laying her heart on the line, she'd secretly hoped Quinn would be thrilled by her confession. Instead, he flung the pen furiously onto the top of the desk and they both watched as it skidded across the wide, polished surface, finally coming to land silently on the thick carpet.

When Quinn returned his gaze to Jessica's, his eyes had hardened to stone. Jessica was forced to consider the unpleasant fact that she might be too late.

"Damn you, Jessie O'Neill," he growled on a harsh breath. "Why didn't you tell me? Why did you drive me crazy all these past weeks?"

She shook her head, feeling duly chastised. "I was afraid."

"Of me?" His tone was incredulous. "I told you from the beginning how I felt about you. How in blue blazes could you think I'd do anything to hurt you?"

"You were going to marry Pamela Stuart," Jessica felt obliged to point out, lifting her chin bravely. "You didn't think that would hurt me?"

He muttered a soft oath. "For an intelligent woman, you sure can be some dumb female." As he dragged his fingers through his hair, Jessica noticed his hands were shaking. "What in the hell am I going to do with you?"

It was now or never. Putting her feelings for Quinn before her pride, Jessica slowly rose from the chair, moving around the vast expanse of oak separating them and settled herself boldly onto his lap. Encouraged by the fact that he didn't toss her to the floor, she twined her arms around his neck.

"If you're open to suggestions," she said softly, nuzzling his ear, "I've got one or two to offer."

The muscles in his shoulders began to relax. He put his arms around her waist. "Doing a little plea bargaining, counselor?"

"Could be," she agreed with a tantalizing smile that faded as her expression turned inordinately serious. "Quinn, will you marry me?"

He paused, as if the decision were a particularly difficult one.

Her heart was beating too fast. Jessica felt as if she'd run up a steep flight of stairs. She waved her hand in front of his face.

"Quinn?"

He shook his head slightly, as if to clear it. "Sorry, Jess. It's just that I've never had a woman propose to me before."

The waiting was driving her crazy. If this was what men went through when they proposed, it was amazing that the institution of matrimony had survived all these generations.

"Well?" she asked, unwilling to wait a moment longer for Quinn's answer.

A broad grin split his face. "Sweetheart, I thought you'd never ask!"

His lips covered hers in a long, lingering kiss that neither participant was eager to end. Finally Quinn broke the intimate contact, resting his chin atop Jessica's head.

"Thank you, Pam," he murmured, unaware he'd spoken out loud until Jessica's head suddenly jerked up.

"It's not what you're thinking," Quinn said instantly, soothingly.

"How do you know what I'm thinking?"

"I can venture a guess."

"Try."

Quinn shifted Jessica on his lap, eyeing her warily. "You're thinking that I've got a helluva nerve saying some other woman's name after I've just accepted your proposal."

"I'm sure you've got a marvelous explanation," Jessica responded calmly, secure in the knowledge that it was she Quinn loved and not Pamela.

"I do want to marry you, Jessica. It's all I've wanted from that first moment I saw you standing in the doorway of the ballroom, looking as delectable as a strawberry ice-cream cone in that pink running suit."

Quinn saw Jessica's eyes soften at the memory of that night. Encouraged, he continued. "You have to understand, I was desperate. I was going crazy without you in my arms, in my bed . . . But most of all, I needed you in my life."

Comprehension slowly dawned, and Jessica stared at Quinn in amazement. "Pamela planted that story, didn't she? She played the same role for you that you've always played for her. It was all a hoax!"

"I'm afraid so," he admitted. "I didn't want to hurt you, Jess. I only wanted you to realize how right we were for each other. How we belonged together."

His tanned face appeared heartbreakingly vulnerable. Jessica didn't know whether to kiss him or hit him over the head with the nearest blunt object.

"How did you know I'd see the paper? I normally don't even read the society page."

"I didn't think Vanessa would miss an opportunity to show it to you. I've never been one of her favorite people."

"You were once," Jessica felt obliged to point out.

Quinn shook his head. "Vanessa made more of that than I expected. I never promised her anything, Jessica. I told her from the start about my goals. And at that point in time they never included marriage."

"I suppose I'm lucky I met you after your fortieth birthday," Jessica murmured, a sad little note creeping into her voice.

His eyes darkened with a loving gleam. "Believe me, Jess, if I'd been fortunate enough to have run into you during those days, all my good intentions would have gone flying out the window."

"Really?" she asked, tracing the hard line of his jaw.

"Really," he confirmed, turning his head to press a kiss against her fingertips. "We were made for each other, sweetheart. Timing had nothing to do with it."

Her misgivings dissolved, Jessica snuggled against him. "Quinn?"

"Mmm?"

"What would you have done if I hadn't come to your office today?"

"I was going to give you twenty-four hours, then kidnap you and keep you hostage in my bed until you agreed to marry me," he replied promptly.

"I've already agreed to marry you," she told him. "In fact, for the record, I did the proposing."

Quinn knew what an effort it had taken for Jessica to put aside her pride and come to his office today. He couldn't remember loving her more than he did at this moment.

His eyes brightened with a seductive gleam. "It's still not such a bad idea. I especially like the part about keeping you hostage in my bed."

"Kidnapping's a capital offense."

"Ah, but I was hoping I could convince a certain sexy assistant D.A. not to press charges."

"I couldn't neglect my duties, Quinn. Even for you." She gave him a sensual little smile. "Of course, if you're willing to plead guilty, I could probably get you released to my custody."

"How long a sentence are they handing out for kidnapping these days?"

"It's a very serious charge, Quinn. I'd say fifty years to life, at the very least."

Quinn's answering grin wreathed his handsome face and lines fanned out from those brilliant emerald eyes she had not been able to put from her mind during their time apart.

"Fifty years to life," he agreed between kisses. "At the very least."

Harlequin Temptation

COMING NEXT MONTH

Can you keep a secret?

You can keep this one plus 4 free novels

WORLDWIDE LIBRARY IS YOUR TICKET TO ROMANCE, ADVENTURE AND EXCITEMENT

Experience it all in these big, bold Bestsellers— Yours exclusively from WORLDWIDE LIBRARY WHILE QUANTITIES LAST